The Traveling Tide

Conversation Pieces

A Small Paperback Series from Aqueduct Press
Subscriptions available: www.aqueductpress.com

About the Aqueduct Press Conversation Pieces Series

The feminist engaged with sf is passionately interested in challenging the way things are, passionately determined to understand how everything works. It is my constant sense of our feminist-sf present as a grand conversation that enables me to trace its existence into the past and from there see its trajectory extending into our future. A genealogy for feminist sf would not constitute a chart depicting direct lineages but would offer us an ever-shifting, fluid mosaic, the individual tiles of which we will probably only ever partially access. What could be more in the spirit of feminist sf than to conceptualize a genealogy that explicitly manifests our own communities across not only space but also time?

Aqueduct's small paperback series, Conversation Pieces, aims to both document and facilitate the "grand conversation." The Conversation Pieces series presents a wide variety of texts, including short fiction (which may not always be sf and may not necessarily even be feminist), essays, speeches, manifestoes, poetry, interviews, correspondence, and group discussions. Many of the texts are reprinted material, but some are new. The grand conversation reaches at least as far back as Mary Shelley and extends, in our speculations and visions, into the continually-created future. In Jonathan Goldberg's words, "To look forward to the history that will be, one must look at and retell the history that has been told." And that is what Conversation Pieces is all about.

L. Timmel Duchamp

Jonathan Goldberg, "The History That Will Be" in Louise Fradenburg and Carla Freccero, eds., *Premodern Sexualities* (New York and London: Routledge, 1996)

Conversation Pieces
Volume 5

The Traveling Tide

Short Fiction

by

Rosaleen Love

Published by Aqueduct Press
PO Box 95787
Seattle, WA 98145-2787
www.aqueductpress.com

ISBN: 978-0-974655-99-4

Cover and Book Design by Kathryn Wilham
Original Block Print of Mary Shelley by Justin Kempton:
www.writersmugs.com

Cat's Eye Nebula (p 60)
NASA Hubble Telescope Images
STScI-2004-27
Credit: NASA, ESA, HEIC, and the Hubble Heritage Team
(STScI/AURA)

Coral drawings by Brigid Cole-Adams © 2004 (pp 46, 54)
Beach photo by Thomas Duchamp © 2005 (p 20)

Acknowledgments

"Alexander's Feats," *Eidolon*, 25/26, Spring 1997, pp. 59-68.

"Ursula K. Le Guin and Therolinguistics" *Paradoxa. Studies in World Literary Genres,* 4 (9) 1998, pp. 231-236.

"The Shadow of the Stones," In Bill Congreve (ed) *Southern Blood: New Australian Tales of the Supernatural,* Sandglass Press, 2003, pp. 166-173.

"Bubbles in the Cosmic Saucepan," *Arena Magazine,* 5, June-July 1993. Reprinted in *Changing Life. Genomes. Ecologies. Bodies. Commodities,* eds Peter J Taylor et al., University of Minnesota Press, Minneapolis, 1997, pp. 196-202.

"Once Giants Roamed the Earth" published simultaneously here and in *Daikaiju! Giant Monster Tales,* edited by Robert Hood and Robin Pen, Agog! Press, 2005.

*The tide of time flow'd back with me
The forward-flowing tide of time*
—Tennyson

This book is for Harold, who, upon being asked for ideas for an epigraph, thought for two seconds, and from the depths of his prodigious memory produced two lines of verse that says it all.

Contents

Alexander's Feats

This is the untold story of Alexander, the Great Man of Science. You may have heard of Alexander the Great, Man of Conquest. But man of genius and invention? Conqueror of space and time? A man who found the secret of eternal youth and gave it to his wife?

The genius of Alexander worked by trial and error, through observation and experiment. He found the trick of it and left it to others after him to flesh out details of the theory.

Some knowledge is hidden still.

How Alexander gave his beloved wife Roxanne
the secret of eternal youth, though he never could tell what it was that he did.

One day Alexander, propped on a single, regal elbow, looked closely at his wife who slept beside him.

"How sorry I am for you!" he whispered into her soft pink ear.

Roxanne tilted her fair head so she could hear more clearly.

"All women have a problem."

Roxanne knew it. *Men!* Still she pretended to sleep.

Alexander sighed. "Women grow old."

Roxanne took heed. Would Alexander take another wife?

Alexander paused. "Of course, men, too, grow old. Not me. I am the son of a god and hence immortal."

Roxanne was on her guard. She would keep watch on Alexander. He was about to stray. Again.

❄

It was winter, the time when armies rested and recovered their strength for the summer of conquest lying ahead. Winter was the season that civilized nations devote to archery and the care of animals. Winter was the time Alexander took for his experiments.

Roxanne was at her wits end. "Not tonight," she said firmly, eyeing the latest herbal draught that was placed before her.

"Why my dear wife, Roxanne, do you not wish to stay young forever?"

"I do, my King."

"Why then, drink this potion of eternal youth."

"My belly aches. It will not be good for me, to take it at this time of month."

"This draught is from herbs that grow in the valleys of Mir Samir. The lamas praise them as herbs of rare virtue and power."

"If I drink, I shall grow a beard. And then I shall lose your love."

"Come now!"

"I am quite convinced of it. The lamas have beards so long they tie them in knots and toss them over their shoulders."

"But they are men already! A beard means nothing in those circumstances."

"How do you know for sure?"

"It's called an experiment," said Alexander. "I shall not know for certain until after the event."

"Then it will be too late, for you shall have a bearded, ageless wife." Roxanne burst into tears.

"I know it is that time of the month," Alexander soothed. "I shall drink the potion myself, and you shall see it cannot hurt you."

Alexander drank the potion, but his act neither confirmed nor denied Roxanne's worst fears. For he was already a man with a beard, and immortal besides.

But Roxanne's words gave him food for thought. The men of the mountains, the lamas, possess many strange powers. They claim to be able to hover above the earth, not touching it. They sit naked in snow, and the heat of their bodies melts ice.

And what of the Syrian bear? It sleeps the winter away and emerges refreshed in the spring. It lives a long life, that bear.

Alexander sent his men to find a bear and kill it.

Roxanne looked at the new potion Alexander had prepared for her. "Are you suggesting, my lord, that if I drink this I shall sleep all winter?"

"Like the bear, you will reawaken in the fine first flurry of your youth!"

"If I slept all winter, you would take a second wife! And I would be rejected!"

"What if I did take a second wife?" he replied. "She would sleep all summer, and you two need never meet."

There was no end to Roxanne's objections.

And when she heard what was in his latest potion! "Entrails of bear?" she screeched.

Once more Alexander muttered dark things and drank the concoction himself. He roistered for three days and nights without ceasing, and his stools turned a luminous green.

The herbalist was banished to the mountains.

When Alexander recovered his temper he realized that something strange had happened. He had come back to his senses after three days without knowing time had passed. Something had worked, in some way, in that potion.

Alexander kept up his search for the secret of youth. "There is this country," he told Roxanne. "It is the country which lies just beyond this place. I am told that the women who live there die at the beginning of winter. They are buried, and in spring their coffins are opened. They step out, young and beautiful again!"

Roxanne refused to think about it. Indeed, Alexander could see that the experiment had it dangers. He would not perform it on himself. And the ethics of the situation would not allow him to test it on his wife.

One night, on the first day of winter, Roxanne disappeared. That night she slept by his side. The next morning when he woke, she was gone. Alexander searched for her everywhere. He grieved for her, believing her slain by his enemies.

Six months later she ran screaming from the cave of the Syrian bear. She came back with no recollection of the passing of time and with her youth restored to her.

Alexander was off on his campaigning, but news of her return soon reached him. He sent for her, rejoicing in his heart.

All Roxanne could say was that she fell asleep in one place and awoke in another, her head on the warm fur of a Syrian cub.

"Bears!" said Alexander, "I always knew they had something to do with it!"

Roxanne vowed never to have anything to do with a bear for the rest of her life.

Alexander promised to stop his experiments. "One test is enough to establish the point. I put some herbs into your drink. They must have done the trick."

"You never said!" Roxanne liked what she saw each morning in the mirror. Secretly, though, she doubted it had been Alexander's doing. Her father Darius the King had gone to war believing himself to be an agent of Light against the powers of Darkness.

"See the world before your eyes," Darius told the infant Roxanne. "You are a small part of the great war of the cosmos waged at the level of the Truth and the Lie. The battle will go on for ever and ever, at all levels of the cosmos, each side seeking to ensnare and conquer the other."

Darius, being a King, saw himself in the grip of wild cosmic forces far greater than himself. Roxanne, being a woman, knew the forces of men were the forces she must reckon with.

"And besides," Roxanne told Alexander, "it was not quite the way my father said. It seemed to me that for that winter, I passed for one short night from the kingdom of light into the kingdom of darkness. But it was not an evil, just a different place. Time passed more swiftly there."

"It must have been the entrails of the bear," said Alexander.

Roxanne knew better than to contradict him.

How Alexander invented the bathyscape and descended to the bottom of the Caspian Sea and founded a new Alexandria among the fish.

It was an invention that took all his ingenuity. He dreamed of a machine and tried to make it with stout timbers and proud beams of oak. But the caulking did not hold. The wooden sphere plunged into the sea and sank, as planned. But the trickle of water through the caulking soon turned into a gush, and Alexander had to make a swift and far from elegant escape.

Roxanne arrived swiftly at the scene to soothe his fevered brow, but her loving care was not enough.

Alexander sat on a cliff and brooded. He took to drinking red wine in large amounts. What if the kingdom of the sea should be beyond his reach? It was unthinkable that he should accept this first defeat if he was to conquer all. He sent to Egypt for sweet-smelling powder to anoint his body.

Roxanne feared the worst. Soon Alexander would blame her for his defeat. His moods took on new urgency for her. How could she endure his frustration for all eternity?

Roxanne consulted a soothsayer but learned nothing. The soothsayer spoke in cryptic riddles, as was his custom, especially when asked questions by a Queen about a King.

Alexander called for more goatskins of good red wine. He took to sitting on his rocky crag and drinking. The vapors of the wine rose up around him.

One day a fierce storm whipped up. Lightning flashed to earth. Alexander took no notice, lost as he was to the world in the oblivion of drink. Roxanne sent a warrior to bring him back to safety. But as the warrior ran to do his task, a bolt of lightning fell from the sky.

A sphere of light surrounded Alexander, and he woke and looked around him in amazement.

Roxanne watched in horror as the light gathered Alexander to itself, then gently rolled him down the hill and into the waters of the Caspian Sea. Drunk though he was, Alexander could still see this was an opportunity he must seize. "I am immortal," he later told the story, "and what goes down must rise." He smiled as the waters closed over his sea-craft and thanked his father Jupiter for his divine intervention.

With the sphere of light enclosing him, he sank into the depths. Yet he was neither burned nor drowned.

He bent space with light and created a craft to take him on his travels. He sank into the sea on a golden throne of light.

"Look!" his men cried when he returned. "See how he tames the light! See how he harnesses the storm!"

Alexander said: "The light shone forth from my chariot into the darkness. I saw ruined cities and tall columns of stone. I saw lions that once had stood on the sides of the throne of Nebuchadnezzar, now sunk into the depths. The fish came to pay me homage. I conquered the depths of the sea. Now I must move on."

Confronted with a puzzle of nature, Alexander summoned his philosopher, Aristotle. "I see my travels under the sea as a sign of my divinity. Surely these are not the forces of nature at work, but the workings of a god?"

"Just how many goatskins of wine did you drink?" asked Aristotle.

"Five only."

"You may be right," said Aristotle. "But in my experience it is best to look first for the causes of things in the forces of nature before bringing in the gods."

"What would you say?"

"A sphere of fire formed about you," he said. "Perhaps it was a fire that forms in the mines deep in the earth, a fire that glows but is cool to the touch. It rises sometimes to the surface. It fell upon you, and you chose to roll with it into the water. You accepted it as a chariot your father Jupiter had created for you."

"If fire rises to its natural place high in the heavens, how was it that I sank?"

"With you at its center, it grew heavy and sank into the sea.

"How come I rose again?"

"Ah, there you have me."

"My father, Jupiter, caused that to happen."

"I grant that, but I would suggest that he chose to work through the forces of nature, as even gods must sometimes do."

"What next?"

"After your fall, you rose again, expelled back to the realm of air, your natural place."

"I swear to you, I saw the heavens part, and Jupiter looked down on me."

Aristotle conceded defeat. Alexander traveled beneath the water, but it was left to others later to establish the true causes of that effect.

✸

They said of Alexander that after he conquered Persia, he became soft, in the Persian manner, and by this they meant he was seduced by their soft and luxurious way of living, enamored of strong wines, soft silks, sweet music, silk pantaloons. They said that he ordered all who approached him to bow low and grovel in the dirt. He sent camels to Egypt, they said, for expensive oils for massage and for his favorite powder for use in wrestling.

Another story might be told, of Alexander the man who believed divine power favored him, who, through knowledge of his supernatural origin, came to appreciate all the more the natural beauties of this earth. He was a King who judged it his responsibility to partake of all the pleasures of this world in order to know it more surely, treasure it more dearly. Only then could he move on to explore new kingdoms in the stars.

Of Roxanne, his wife, not so many stories have been told, which is the point of this present chronicle. Behind every great Emperor and every great inventor, there lies the springs of genius, genius that may be original, but that often lies in the actions and ideas of an unacknowledged other.

It is to Roxanne that true credit must be given for Alexander's last, most marvelous invention. For it was Roxanne who discovered the secret of interstellar travel and gave it to her man.

How Roxanne discovered the secret of interstellar travel and bestowed it on her lord, the Emperor Alexander.

"Is this the great Sea at the Edge of the World?" asked Alexander, when he reached the China Sea. His arrival caused consternation among the local inhabitants. His great army was hungry and needed to be fed.

The great scholar Hsuan-Tsang gestured towards the glittering sea. "It is a great sea, and it is the edge of the world," he agreed. "Need you know more?"

"Then I have conquered to the ends of the earth!" Alexander was first exultant, then his brow creased with sorrow. "But there is nothing left to conquer! I have come to the end of it all."

Hsuan-Tsang was the wisest of men. His face was as round as the evening moon, his cheeks as rosy as the evening mists. Alexander's bronzed face was scarred, his eyes imperious and aggressive.

"The problem is one of geometry," Alexander explained, drawing a circle on the sand.

Roxanne listened intently.

"You see this circle? Now I expand my conquests." Alexander drew a larger circle round the smaller. "You see the problem?"

Roxanne saw the void space that lay beyond the boundary. Hsuan-Tsang frowned.

"It is a question of ever-expanding boundaries to my empire. It is a question of the ever-increasing difficulty in keeping those ever-increasing boundaries secure. That is why I see things the way I do. I propose a simple solution. I dream of having no borders, no boundaries to my conquest. Security lies here, geometry lies there. Uniting the two, that is the trick of it. I see a borderless kingdom, with the whole world now one great Alexandria. The whole world, under my rule, under my eternal rule."

"Only the one world?" murmured the great Chinese sage.

Roxanne looked at him sharply.

Alexander was puzzled. "You tell me I have come to the end of the world."

"This is the Great Sea, and it is the Edge of the World," Hsuan-Tsang agreed. "But look at the stars, and see what other worlds there are for you to conquer! An infinity of worlds—and all for you!"

Alexander wept. How could he conquer all those other worlds that twinkled so brightly at night in the heavens?

"There is a problem with this particular world, with this particular sea. The world is round, and there is no edge to it, as you imagine. If you set sail on this sea, you will return one way or the other: you will travel across the water and sooner or later you will come back to the country from which you began your travels."

Alexander grunted at the wildness of this notion. Who would set out on his travels only to arrive at the place he had left? Step up to the stars, though, to go on in eternal conquest: that was a better idea.

"There is a beginning, and a middle, but where there seems to be an end, there then is only another beginning," the wisest of men remarked.

Alexander brightened at the thought.

Roxanne grew gloomy. She looked up at the stars and knew she wanted, above all else, to stay warm and comfortable at home. She questioned her man. "What if I were to tell you I do not want to come with you?"

Alexander was generous. "I do not ask that of you. I ask only that you stay faithful until my return."

Roxanne looked at the stars and at the sheer number of them. "It will take a long time," she said, calculating.

"It is in my nature," said Alexander. "I cannot do otherwise."

"Then it is my duty to help you."

Roxanne took Hsuan-Tsang aside and spoke quietly to him. "What has wings and can fly through the air?"

"An eagle?"

"What has wings and can fly through the air with a man on its back?"

"I confess, I do not know."

"What if the eagle had the body of a lion and the strength of ten oxen and wings which could bear half an army aloft?"

Hsuan-Tsang responded with a problem of his own. "I dreamed last night of a lotus that was made from the hardest stone and dwelt in the depths of the sea. A fierce storm blew up and cast the lotus at my feet. Each time I tried to grasp it, the lotus retreated from me."

Roxanne smiled. "I know what you want to know. Find me a griffin and I shall tell you. If a griffin were to bear Alexander aloft, who knows where he might come down? Go to Bactria in my father's lands, and tell them Roxanne sent you." Griffins have secrets that only Roxanne knew.

Summer gave way to winter and thence to spring. The time of retreat to archery and the care of animals had passed. Alexander yearned to travel on.

"The time has come," said Hsuan-Tsang. "Come with me, and I shall show you the way." Roxanne's heart leapt. This was the moment she had been waiting for.

They walked towards the shore, where warriors were lined up in formation. Each man held a long thread that reached up into the sky, so high that the kites flying above, if kites they were, seemed mere specks in the sky. At a signal the soldiers pulled in their threads. There, spiraling, tumbling, swooping down the sky came a crowd of the most elegant griffins. Down they swooped through the air to sit at the feet of their new master.

The griffins were half lion, half eagle. Their heads and wings were those of the eagle, burnished with gold. Their bodies were covered in soft long golden fur. The light of the stars flashed from their black eyes. Their ears stood in sharp points. Deep red jewels glowed on their studded collars and their golden reins.

"Take these griffins as tribute to you, my lord, from the Emperor of China to the Emperor of the rest of the world!"

Alexander was delighted. He had come to the end of this world, but there would be other worlds to conquer.

Roxanne marveled at the sight. "I knew these griffins in my father's country. Fine animals all; they deserve better than this terrible fate, to rise only while chained to this earth. Take these griffins and fly, for they will take you where you want to go."

Alexander looked doubtful.

"I shall show you." Roxanne called for a griffin to be saddled and brought to her. Then from round her neck she took a silver purse. The griffin stiffened with excitement. The chain was severed and she rode towards the sky. The griffin looked back over its shoulder at Roxanne and at the silver purse she wore around her neck. Then its eyes filled with the light of the stars and the tears of the wanderer who finds, at last, the true path home. Roxanne smiled, and leaned forward to stroke the animal's soft ears. She opened the purse. The griffin pricked its ears in the air; its nostrils quivered; its neck grew strong and straight. Then, in full sight of Alexander and his army, Roxanne and her beast both disappeared.

Alexander cursed himself for his stupidity. How could he let Roxanne fall into such danger? Once more he mourned his lost wife.

But not for long. Soon there was another commotion, and Roxanne reappeared in the skies. She rode her proud griffin back upon the sands. "Look," she cried, as she flung down before Alexander a branch of a glittering gold, "See what I have brought you! Here is the secret of travel to the stars!"

"What happened, Roxanne?"

"Griffins will bear you aloft and take you where you want to go."

That last night there was much feasting and laughter, and sorrow and anticipation of the pangs of parting.

Later, Alexander asked Roxanne, "Tell me, how do you know these things?"

"See how the griffin sniffs the air, drinking in smell. What is the sense of smell but the act of perceiving small particles borne from one place to another upon the ethereal wind? There is a strong power of attraction of the bird for this herb, as strong as the earth for the stone that lies upon it, as strong as the water for the earth that lies beneath it, as strong as the air for the water that lies beneath it in its turn, and as strong as the fire for the air that lies underneath. Such is the power of attraction that like will fly to like in the twinkling of an eye. You will cross to the stars and continue on your way. It is all perfectly logical."

"Why then, you are a true philosopher. I shall part from Aristotle and take you with me!"

Roxanne shook her head.

Alexander turned to Hsuan-Tsang. "Will you come with me to the stars?"

"No. I have entered this troubled whirl of death and birth here, upon this earth. It is this world to which I belong and to which I must return—life after death, death after life."

"I have the gift of eternal life," Alexander replied. "Eternity—indeed, infinity—is no problem to me. If there is one life and that one life is eternal, then the precept of reincarnation is irrelevant." Alexander stroked the griffin's soft flank. Its beak swiveled round. Its sharp eyes followed his movement. Then it let out a deep soft purr, like a cat. "In Bactria, they told me that griffins guard the treasures of the Kings. In all my time in Bactria I never saw them. But now, I have come to the end of the world, and here they await me."

"Be vigilant, my griffins," commanded Alexander. "Take me to the stars!" The griffins chirruped. They hauled Alexander and his men aloft.

Swiftly they rose through the sphere of air to where the fifth essence of matter, the *quinta-essentia,* grows in power and influence. The griffins grew wild with joy. It is from the *quinta-essentia* that fabulous beings take their power of life and chief source of motion, the divine fuel that powers them to the remote reaches of the heavens, without benefit of crossing the distance in between. Arrival is in a moment of time.

Alexander ascended and found new worlds to conquer.

A long time ago Alexander defeated the Persian King Darius and wed his daughter Roxanne. The two Kings had gone to war, each believing in his heart that he served the truth. But truth to tell, they were but minor players in the cosmic battle between the forces of the Truth and the Lie. Both held themselves on the side of Truth and thus helped to serve the Lie.

Wars of domination and conquest exist at all levels of creation. At the human level, all is muddle and confusion.

Hsuan-Tsang dispatched the conqueror Alexander from his shores without the necessity for fighting. Then he turned to Roxanne and said, "I brought your griffins. Now you must tell me what you know about my dream."

"All dreams signify something," said Roxanne. "Nothing is in vain. You dreamed of a lotus. His dream was of the stars."

Roxanne showed Hsuan-Tsang the path back through all the dominions Alexander had conquered. Neither were interested in taking great treasure, nor was it their intention to conquer all the world. They knew that to win these things in this life was to lose them in the next.

But with that notion Alexander would never have agreed, and so it was best that they had parted from him.

In the Shadow of the Stones

It is the earth's crust which engulfs.
That which seems solid, melts, then re-forms, careless,
indifferent, unaware. The sea turns to fire.
The earth is solid. It opens.
Air is fluid: it refuses to grant passage.
Fire freezes.

❦

Have you noticed that people who once used to be
very important to you no longer seem to be around?
It happens gradually. One year it seems you are almost
living in each other's houses, you are so close. You
go to see films together, or jog along the river bank.
Then something happens, or perhaps nothing really
definite happens that you can point to and say, that
was what happened, that was the moment of parting.
You just drift away and apart. Gradually the times between meetings grows longer and then, why, you say to
yourself, its been years since I last saw Jenny or Judith
or Posy.

Must be getting philosophical in my old age, Queenie
thought. Then the next thought to come along was,

"How old *am* I?" That thought got the shove, quick smart. She didn't want all that stuff in her head. She needed to *feel* more about Jenny and Rachel and Posy. Then she'd make the effort to see them, ask them round. Except Posy—can't ask him. Oh, that hurt, how it hurt. Queenie curled herself up into a ball in her bed until the sadness passed. As it does, as it does.

Then Gordon rang to say that Shelley was gone. Disappeared. Queenie cried. "Shelley! Not Shelley! It's all my fault. I didn't care enough. Oh Shelley! You were so lovely!"

First it was Rachel, whom Queenie scarcely knew. Then the others. They disappeared without a trace. The pattern was—no pattern. Random occurrences. No connections. Except in the nature of the women. Their loveliness. And the men? They were in the company of the women at the time.

Queenie was sad and not at all beautiful, while Shelley, oh Shelley was so lovely, and that was why she was chosen, of that Queenie had no doubt. There just had to be something in the meeting of their opposites, her sorrow with Shelley's happiness. While Shelley, had she been asked before she disappeared, wouldn't even have been able to put a name to Queenie. She was just another one of those quiet, mousy girls on the fringe of her set.

North, Shelley had gone north with a bunch of friends. Queenie rang up everyone she knew who went on that fateful trip. "Where did you go? What did you do? What did you see? What happened first? What happened next?" Until they said, "Lay off it, Queenie. Can't you see we're still upset?"

"I shall go where she went, do what she did, live as she lived. I shall think of her every minute of every day. I shall never forget her. I shall send vibes from my innermost being. I shall call out to her."

Queenie borrowed a car. George was away. He wouldn't mind. She drove north to the place where Shelley had disappeared.

They'd stopped that night, the group, at the place where pinnacles of rock dotted the desert sand like so many thousands of termite mounds crowding over the hills to the sea. "It was all a terrible mistake," Shelley's friends told Queenie before they stopped talking to her. "We didn't mean to stay there. It was just a spur-of-the-moment thing. If we hadn't, if we'd just gone straight up as we planned, then we'd still have Shelley." Queenie planned carefully. Her trip. Water. Sleeping bag. Maps. Hammer. Shovel. Hat jammed hard on her head to keep her hair from going all over the place. Spare hat.

She camped that night in a hollow in the sand and tried her best to sleep. Not knowing, dreaming that Shelley was here and not here, slipping in and out of her dream and drifting into sand and sea and air. If she opened her eyes she saw the rocks, heard the sea in the distance, felt the soft breeze lifting her hair. Solid, rock solid. No space for gaps, for emptiness, for absence, for transparency, for lightness, for that final step into air. Shelley. Not knowing where, not knowing what, not knowing how. Only knowing then, here, something had happened.

The pinnacles march over the hills to the sea.
From vents deep under the sea bubbles of gas
plop up to the surface.   Shelley walks on the
beach, away from her friends. She takes out
a surreptitious cigarette. Bubbles of gas drift
over the sea and onto the land, and as Shelley walks and strikes a light she is caught in
a bubble of inflammable gas, and the flame
sparks and the bubble ignites. Whoosh, Shelley is caught and turns and tries to run, but
the flames are all around her and they burn
and they burn and...and all that is left in the
end is a pile of grey ash that is washed away
by the tide. Meteors fall from the sky. Pum-
ice stone rains down from the eruptions from
distant volcanoes. Ash from bush fires falls on
the beach. Lightning flashes. The earth groans.

Shelley has disappeared. Queenie sleeps fitfully.
The earth has taken its own. Queenie half wakes and
groans. No, no. It wasn't like that. It didn't happen
that way.

Deep under the sea the ocean floor shakes
and quakes, and vibrations build and build
until the sea gathers its own, its water, and
the sea on the shore is sucked back and goes
far out so quickly that the locals know that
something is amiss, but the visitor strolling
along the shoreline is oblivious of danger,
until—whoosh—water sweeps in with one
large rolling wave that races way up the beach
and claims the unwitting walker for its own.

Tsunami! Shelley is walking along the shore, and a freak wave comes, and she is knocked over, her head bashed into the sands. The waters rush over her, she passes into unconsciousness and is swept away into death.

The others though, the other women who have disappeared. The pattern, the link, between Shelley who was here and others who were elsewhere when they vanished. If there is pattern. The unknown clouds of bubbles of subterranean gas, the freak waves that reach far inland, the earth that opens beneath the feet of young, beautiful, talented women, the gap into which they step, not knowing, the earth opens, a chasm; they fall into the chasm, the earth closes and…Or there is a serial killer who knows how to dispose of the remains. Completely dispose of them. Queenie shivers and asks, "What is truth, shall I get to know it, do I want to know, and what if, what if…and why, why now, after so long, am I awakening into the life of pain and sorrow once more?"

Judith disappeared in Perth. She walked out one evening to get some milk. Queenie brushed against her that last day. Judith never returned home. A tidal wave in Murdoch, pockets of subterranean gas bubbling up from the basement of the milk-bar, chasms in the pavement, a murderer lurking in the alley with a knife, a mincing machine, a crocodile (salt-water), an acid-bath? Rumors fly. There are so many ways to vanish without trace.

Queenie sleeps and the earth stirs beneath her. The pinnacles of stone stand guard. Soldiers stand guard and watch. Those pinnacles were watching all right. They were watching Queenie. She wakes suddenly. She is not in her flat. She is caught tight in a bed-roll while some nameless phantom runs shrieking in her dream, getting closer and closer, and still she can't move. She gathers her body, ready to spring. She half-opens her eyes.

Nobody. Only the pinnacles. And in the distance, two men stirring in swags in the shadow of their van. She is not the only camper. That's all. Nothing to worry about. Best that way, in fact. Not to be alone. To be among tourists. Queenie gets up, stretches, yawns, and ambles down the hill to the beach.

Under the sea, bubbles of gas gather and rise to the surface. The pinnacles march to the edge of the sea and disappear. But where they seem to end they do not really vanish. They go subterranean, marching underground all the way to Perth, pinnacle spires of rock within rock, rock that is hard within rock that is soft, columns of underground rock deep in the cathedral of the earth, pinnacles rising amid the gravel and the unconsolidated crumbling of other rocks.

Underneath Perth there is another city...the city of pinnacles.

The roadside cutting in Perth, that's where Queenie first saw them, the pinnacles. She'd stopped her bike once, there, though it was dangerous, the lane being marked with double white lines. Queenie stood and admired the shapes rock takes within rock. "Like a city within a city," she thought. "Except to live there, you must be a different kind of person, you must lack substance, possess instead an incorporeity that will stand you in good stead in that most corporeal of worlds, to float into the rock, to mingle your substance with rock. They would float through rock as we float through air into water. It's the way things are for them."

That was where she met Jenny and Phil. Briefly. They stopped their bikes beside hers, closer to the safety of the rock face. Queenie stood in the middle of the road, paying no attention to the cars that screeched around her, honking.

Queenie showed Jenny. "There's a city in there. Look and you can see it. Struts and pillars and floors and roofs and tunnels. A fortress with buttresses and ramparts. Look and you can see."

"Feeling OK?" asked Jenny. She peered from under her black helmet. "Hey, you on something?"

"You do this often?" asked Phil. "Stand in the middle of the road?"

"The rock. The road. I can see it all."

"Come away."

Queenie leaned against the rock, running her fingers down the cool roughness of the stone.

Jenny got on her bike. "I'm off."

"Stoned," Phil mouthed at Jenny.

Queenie pushed back from the face of the rock, her hat catching and falling.

Above them the skies darkened. Rain began to fall.

"Shit," says Jenny, "What's that foul smell?"

The skies will rain down rock and ash. Water will seep into the earth, and Perth will wash away. The underground city of pinnacles will grow to the light.

Queenie is close, oh so close to it, the subterranean world, the world of primeval power. "We are all stoned," she said.

Jenny screamed. Phil was gone. The earth shook. The screaming stopped.

Queenie picked up her hat. There are people who live in the rock. It's not just an empty city in there. She catches a quick glimpse of something and the darkness closes over.

Jenny and Phil have taken a long ride to nowhere. Two bikes lie propped against the rock. There you have it, Queenie tells herself yet again. The people she meets just don't seem to like her very much. She tries her best to be friendly. But it just never seems to work.

Judith wakes, Phil wakes, Jenny wakes. They call out in the darkness. "Help me, help me."

No help comes.

Annie wakes, Rachel wakes. They call out.

No one. Nothing.

The pinnacles are down there, under the ground. Half in, half out, like they're rooted in the sand. They've got roots that go deep down, like teeth have roots that go deep into the jaw. The dentist takes out a tooth and shows you, and you freak out at the blood. Then you see how half the tooth is buried under the skin.

Queenie walks down to the sea. Rachel, Jenny, Judith, Phil even, she hasn't thought of them in a long while. She's looking for Shelley now. The tide is out, and rock-pools are left at the edge of the sea. The surf is far away. Queenie looks to the horizon, whence come freak waves and pockets of subterranean gas. She looks back to the pool and sees water rippling along its surface and a glimpse of something silver in a crevice. She bends over. Why is the water moving like that? When there is no wind, no waves? The earth shakes. It will reclaim its own.

Queenie bends down and tugs at the silver object in the water. It's an earring. Shelley's.

If you know what to look for you can see it, you can feel it; for a moment Queenie thinks she has it near her grasp. The truth. The air is still, the water shakes. She looks for the fireball, the freak wave that will come and take her, the meteor that will drive her dead body deep into the ground. She looks at the earring in her hand, then clasps her fingers tightly around it.

She wasn't here when Shelley disappeared. Shelley had nothing to do with her, nothing at all. She is not responsible. There must be a different reason for Shelley. All vanishings may not be equal. Same ultimate effect, wildly different causes.

Here is a place where land meets sea, where land marches down under the sea in pinnacle fashion.

❦

Deep under the sea the ocean floor quakes and splits. The sea will surge forth and gather its own to itself.

Once there was another story, the story of Queenie and Posy. Posy said he loved her. There were two children. Posy came from across the sea. It was in another place, in another time entirely.

Posy has taken Shelley as he once took Queenie.

Queenie stands at the edge of the sea. She opens her mouth, and a loud, sad wailing *Why?* rises to the skies.

She thought she was safe. There are no safe places. None, never ever. Shelley is a child of the sea, and the sea has reclaimed her. That was the cause of it. Not because Shelly met Queenie and learned to hate her, as all the others have done.

From across the sea Posy had come to Queenie. He came, and she went willingly enough. The sea had whipped to a storm, and Posy came out from the tempest and found her, and together they sought shelter. Posy was cast at her feet, and she ran to him, poor shipwrecked soul, and helped him to stagger up the cliff to a place that promised shelter. Wide doors opened between white stone pillars.

They lay on loose rush matting. Posy became fully a man. His love was as wild as the sea and as warm as the Aeolian winds. Queenie remembered the wind, though his face and whether his hair curled softly down his chest were details lost in the haze. Poseidon loved Queenie for that one moment, and that was all Queenie ever had of love. Athena was furious when she found out, and that was the end of Posy, at least in Queenie's life.

There had been two children, but somewhere along the way they had been lost. Queenie has done terrible things all her long life. No wonder people don't like her much.

Queenie stooped down by the water's edge and picked up a glittering silver loop. The sea shrinks back. A god has awakened from slumber. The sea has gathered its own.

Queenie wears a cap indoors, outdoors, day and night. "I can never do anything with my hair," Queenie tells Rachel. "Nothing at all. It's totally impossible. That's why I don't have any friends."

"Don't be a dickhead, Queenie." Rachel really said that to her once. Some former friend. How those words hurt! Her head is the temple of her soul.

There are worlds within worlds within worlds. The true world is the world within stone. All else is appearance.

Queenie holds the earring tight in her hand. It is her keepsake, something of Shelley's. She has found it.

The horizon. Nothing to see. No ball of burning fire, no incipient tidal wave, no tempest bearing a strange man from another world. Only water quivering in a pool in rock.

The pinnacles did not grow from underneath. Perhaps they fell from the skies. Slabs and slivers of rock plummet down and hit the earth, like fence posts driven deep. The pinnacles were dropped from above. This pattern, which looks like no pattern at all, was planned by someone. Or something.

Posy has come and has taken Shelley. He has taken her as once he took Queenie to a temple cut into the cliff.

Why wasn't Queenie told?

The sea gathers its own and spits them out. The earth takes its own and turns them either to dust or to stone.

They stare at her from stone, the wanderers, the rock engravers. Sailors once shipwrecked, who sought safety on the rocks and find no safety there. Their eyes are open, their ears hear, their bodies feel the cold, oh the cold. Queenie sees them, she sees the rock open before her. Once more she can see the struts and pillars of the underground city.

Underneath Perth there is another city, the city of pinnacles. There Queenie may find her now quite stony friends: Rachel and Judith, Jenny and Phil. One day wind and rain and waters rising from the sea will wear down the present city of Perth, and the forest of petrified people will rise to the air.

Her mother always said, "Never, never leave a trail of bodies behind as you go, Medusa. It's not fair to the people who have to come along after you to clean up." She was always considerate that way. Queenie was just unlucky, that day she was caught in the arms of Poseidon, Athena's betrothed. Athena cursed her. And Queenie turned into the Medusa with snakes for hair, someone whose glance turned those who beheld her to stone.

They say the ancient gods do not ask to be believed. But they want their stories told and retold, again and again. And so the pinnacles march to the edge of the sea and disappear. But where they seem to end they do not really vanish. They go subterranean, marching underground all the way to Perth, pinnacle spires of rock within rock, rock that is hard within rock that is soft, columns of underground rock deep in the cathedral of the earth, pinnacles rising amid the gravels and the unconsolidated crumbling of other rocks.

That which seems solid, melts, then re-forms, careless, indifferent, unaware.

GoGo

1
Paddy's Valley

Paddy's Valley is a place of refuge. Beyond it, sparkling in the heat, lies the grey shale and red soil of the plains, the tough green Spinifex grasses.

Once they were reefs, the hills that fringe the valley. Back reef, marginal slope, and lagoon, you can see them all today once you know what to look for. Note how the lagoon deepens into the bay. That mound is the back reef, and here is the marginal slope, and down there is the bay where once the weird fish swam.

Lloyd Atoll. Wade Knoll. The hills are named from islands. They rise, high and dry and stranded, a jumble of rocks piled between ground and air, all water long since gone. Exposed to air, the back reefs fissured to jagged pinnacles. Soft limestone crumbled to dust. Cave roofs collapsed to earth, and trees now push through crevices in the walls. Fossil shells lie scattered on the ground.

Paddy's Valley gives welcome shelter from the fierce heat of the plain.

Four hundred million years ago, the armour-plated fishes, placoderms, swam along the sandy ocean floor. Now they are found, encased in stone. Pick up the stones, weigh them in your hand, smash them open, and find inside the fossil fish, complete with head and back plates, jaws and skin. This is a place of wonders.

2
375 Million Years Ago: Stunning the Mullet

I've been asked here today to speak of the future of fishes, and I have to say, it's looking rosy for us all. Here we are, the GoGo placoderms, lords of our patch of the Devonian reef. That mob over there, the crinoids, bryozoans, sponges, rugose corals, reef-forming species all, and we need them, as predator needs prey, but they're going nowhere, stuck on the rock, immobile. Fish go where we please. Regard our wide snouts and huge jaws, and our sharp, prominent teeth, so well suited to crunching, crushing, slurping.

Ah, the food-chain. It's a never-ending source of pleasure to us here, on the top.

You've asked me here to talk of higher things, of what placoderms might become, the long-term evolutionary trends. I'm going to push the envelope here. I'm going to think outside the square. Bear with me. Hear me out.

What about considering a radical change in body plan? Fins, and added buoyancy, they'll take us further than before. And ditch the external armor-plated skel-

eton. But crawling out of the sea, up onto the land?
Did you say that? Did my otoliths catch that right? No,
not the way to go. More water than land round here,
except for the odd volcano, and that's not a powerful
incentive for budding legs and walking out on land.

Fishes are highly evolved and deeply spiritual beings. When we die, we may get eaten, true, and that's
the way of the world, but we do try our best to bury
our undigested dead. They sink into the anaerobic
zone, and we go with them, pushing them deep into
the dysaerobic ooze. Silt hardens to stone, and calcium
migrates from bones. Our ancestors are confined each
in their stony nodule, awaiting the world to come.

Envoi:

As for the world to come, nobody knew anything about the Permian mass extinction that
was oncoming, given a hundred million years
or so. Ninety percent of life wiped out—who'd
have seen that coming? Then the land became
the place to be, at least for the dominant
roles. Placoderms, once the fiercest and most
successful group of fish that ever lived, became extinct.

3
The Time Before This Time

Ice Ages come and go. Continents collide, subside,
and rise. Reefs erode, exposed to air, and rise once
more when land tilts underneath the ocean. Ocean and
land shift back and forth. Sea becomes land; land becomes sea.

People came to this land perhaps, who knows, some 30,000 years ago. They came by land, by sea, to this place where good grasses grew on the plains, and the billabong linked to billabong along the valleys, and the animals belonged to the land.

It was the time before this time. Or perhaps it was, is, the time that is still here, but hidden, known only to those who know how to look, what to look for, how to read the land.

In the time before this time, but co-existing with it, giants roamed the earth, half animal, half something else entirely. They came to this place, and they lay down, and look: you can see their features in the hills and their continuing spirit in the waters that flow beneath. These, the first people, will be the last people. They stay on in this place and will never forsake it. In this place—the time before this time, this time, and the time that is to come.

4

1893: Big Paddy and the Valley

There is a story from round these places—the story of Big Paddy.

Imagine an Irishman, far from home, drinking himself to death in the heat and the flies of the valley. That might well be so. But there is another story, of another Paddy, an Aborigine from round these parts. A wild one, Big Paddy; oh, he was wild. The invaders came with their sheep and their cattle, their gift to the country. The year was a dry one. The sheep got away from the paddocks and into the ranges. Big Paddy and his mates went after the sheep, the cattle. It was either that, or starve. It was that bad, that hard dry time. They speared the cattle and ran to the valley, into the caves with roofs open to the sky, labyrinthine. Too far for the police and the settlers, without food for themselves, for their horses. And the ground was too stony, too hard for horses and trackers to follow.

Big Paddy came to this valley. He hid here from the police and the station managers. Not much in the dry, in the valley, in the way of water. Paddy was doing it tough.

The cattle died from spearing. They died caught in bogs. They died giving birth. They died from dog attack. They died from disease. They died from heat and thirst. They died in land set on fire.

The settlers' report:
The natives formed themselves into a hostile camp, burning the country, threatening the settlers, stealing the stock. We had to teach them a severe lesson. We expended 60 rounds of Winchester ammunition.

The natives' report:
The police rushed the camp just before sunrise. We took up spears to defend ourselves and made for the cover of the rocks. The police followed on foot. We threw spears and clubs. The police called for surrender, but we did not know what the word *surrender* meant. When we did not surrender, when we did not give them our spears and our clubs, they took aim with their rifles and shot us. In the early light of morning they fired upon us, and so many died.

Question:
Why is this place called Paddy's Valley?

Answer:
In 1893 Big Paddy and his mob attacked Charlie Blythe at Noonkanbah. Charlie Blythe got away, saved by his Aboriginal workers. Big Paddy fled. He might have come here. Big Paddy got around.

5
1930s: Massacre at Christmas Creek

This comes from the time of the humans, when black humans killed cattle, and white humans killed black humans as payback, and the story goes on and on, this story, for ever and ever and never stops.

Why not start the story again, at another place? The cattle never came. The land was never settled. The Aborigines never killed the cattle. The station managers never shot the Aborigines.

Or: the white men came, and went away again.

Or: the white men came, and sat and listened to the land. They said, this land isn't ours. This land is land that has come from the sea, and one day will return to it, when the oceans rise and cover it once more.

Or: the Aborigines defeated the pastoralists. The pastoralists said: "We see the error of our ways." They cooperated to breed the kanga-sheep and the cow-garoo that comes with milk thickened on the bounce. Soft-footed, these creatures did not harm the land.

These are the stories that didn't happen.

This is the land for which so much blood has been spilt, over and over again, without much point to it. Lives cut short because a man with a gun knew how to use it. The bodies piled high on the wood, doused with kero, the match thrown casually upon the pyre. Nothing is left, no evidence remains. People saw what happened, people knew what the fire was about, but their stories are the stories of women and children, natives, and no-one will ever believe them. The bodies were not buried in graves, but thrown on the flames, and that was the end of that story, of three cattle that got killed, and ten men killed in revenge. The stories go on and on and never stop. If the cattle never came, the men never got killed for them. The land stayed as it was. It never suffered wind-scalds and sheeting, wind-piling and tree-root exposure, and there was no active or passive gullying.

That is a story that is not true.

6
2003: Land Degradation in the Fitzroy Valley of Western Australia

Some of the most severe degradation seen during the survey occurs on the Djada and GoGo land systems. We recommend fencing and stock control, and the ploughing and seeding of the affected country to bring it back into useful production for cattle. The land should be able to support 60,000 cattle units. It currently carries only 26,000.

7
What the Geologist Sees

A dipping fore-reef
with atrypid brachiopods
and a differential dissolution
of the interior of the platform.
On the lee side,
Shale patch and
pinnacle reefs.
A reef platform
with its central part dissolved
leaving a depression with a rim.

8
The Ecotourism Experience

It took all morning for the vehicles to reach the valley. As they bumped down the sandy track, they saw, in the distance, another vehicle departing fast, in the opposite direction.

They reached the valley and discovered why. A pile of nodules lay smashed beside ashes of a still-warm fire. Fossil-smugglers had swept the ancient reef. What the sea has left, the smugglers take.

Garth cursed. Jack got out the radio-phone and notified the boss. Made the official report, though there wasn't anything anyone could do about it.

They were a bunch of tourists on an environmental bender. "Ecotourists tread lightly on the earth," the brochure said. "See the fossil fields of GoGo. At the end of another day in Paradise, refresh yourself in the waters of a cool, refreshing billabong. Christmas Creek invites you in."

Except the last billabong had a resident crocodile, and that was enough to put anyone off a cool, refreshing dip, and the pool was more a mud wallow than a lap-pool. Cassie said, "When you're time's up, it's up." But Cassie did not taunt fate in the form of a croc, once she got a good look at one for the first time.

The brochure said: "Meet with the traditional owners." Traditions change. Judith was surprised to find herself involved in a chat on small business practices and the importance of incentives over hand-outs. It didn't say, in the brochure, meet with the traditional owners of Aboriginal lands and find small business advocates busy pursuing their entrepreneurial skills.

At night the full moon rises, and reef columns cast wild shadows. Bats fly from the caves into moonlight.

During the night they froze, and during the day they dripped with sweat. The heat set in, and hordes of small flies settled on their skin.

"They're not flies," said Gavin. "Entomologically speaking, they're bees."

"Corpse flies," said Hal.

"Why corpse flies?"

"You wouldn't want to know."

Someone, something, dies out here. Flies pick the bones as clean as the bones in the nodules. Wait for the return of the sea and the sedimentary entombing, and become a fossil for the future.

Judith came looking for a real man, and Gavin wasn't it. A real man would fold her in his capacious arms like an angel—a real man would protect her from harm, from old age, from poverty. No way, not here. The man who would protect her forever is in her head and will not get out of it.

Judith was looking for a real man, and Hal wasn't it, either. Hal said a fond goodbye to his wife in Broome and then met Bet. Bet was along as Davy's bit on the side. Davy drove the second vehicle. After two days, Bet's swag moved closer to Hal's as Hal's swag moved further from the campsite, and soon the two were an item and Davy got stuck into the rum well before the sun was up, or down. Davy was a driver. The rum was going to be a problem on the road.

The funny thing was, Hal and Bet thought no one had noticed. Except Davy, of course.

A word of advice: First thing in the morning, roll up your swag and tie it up tight. Otherwise a snake might slither in and curl up in the warmth, and when night comes, when you crawl back into it, you'll be sorry.

9

The Permian Mass Extinction Is a Non-Event

Western Australia is the first and only Australian underwater state. The border to the eastern states has down-faulted along the vertical dividing line, the dotted line on the map.

Tectonic plates now shift and slide under each other according to marks on human maps. The natural links with the political.

Life continues, much as before, though the pastoral industry in the Kimberleys downsized rapidly.

Perth rises on stilts, a Venice of the Antipodes. Tourists come for the gondola experience.

At GoGo, new coral reefs grow from the base of the ancient bryozoan reefs.

And get this. The Permian mass extinction was a non-event for placoderms. Armor-plated fish of all shapes and sizes, from tiddlers to giants, have returned, as if they'd just gone away for a while, somewhere else, somewhere deeper in the unknown ocean, only to come back to their former haunts when the conditions of life improved. At GoGo, fish swim again in the ancient bays, and when they die, their bones settle into the ooze, in this time as in times long past.

Tourists come to snorkel among them, though they must swim protected by large steel cages.

10
Finale

Once reef-building plants and animals filtered light, air, and water, and from these elements, so insubstantial, from blue-green algae, microscopic in size, from nothing, came this place. Light, air, and water. See-moss, bryozoans, sponges, stromatoporoids, nautiloids, ammonites, gastropods. Dead life sank to the bottom of the bay, calcareous skeletons turned to rock. Three hundred million years ago the ocean pounded on the outer edge of the reef. Sunlight filtered through the blue-green shallows. Armor-plated fish swam on the ocean floor. In death, the fish sank deep into sand and wrapped themselves in stone. The waters fell, and the land became swamp, then forest, then desert, then something else.

In the columns of rock, on the floors of the caves, you will see sponges, tabulate and rugose corals, bryozoans, worm-shaped tubes of tentaculoids, crinoids, trilobites, gastropods, bivalves. Ripples of waves long gone are set in limestone. Rillenkarst formations. Fossil waves.

Light, air, and water made this reef. The waters came and went and came again. Light, air, water, and bones have made this place. Now the people are gone. They traveled light, and light as air, they passed away into nothing.

Ursula K. Le Guin and Therolinguistics

We stand on the shoulders of giants, of that there is no doubt, though this phrase is often taken to mean we stand on the shoulders of giant men. In this case, they'd be wrong, for it was Ursula K. Le Guin who single-handedly created the science of therolinguistics, or the study of the language of animals. In "The Author of the Acacia Seeds" (1974) she was the first to decipher the language of ants. But just as linguistic, structuralist analyses have been superseded by poststructuralism and postmodernism, so Le Guin's analysis of Ant has had its day. Therolinguistics as a description, *however brilliant*, of a small group of Ant sentences is no longer enough. Nor is it the aim of the therolinguistics game to achieve the grand meta-narrative of Ant in piecing together sentence fragments to spell out even as singular a story as Le Guin has told. The move is, as David Harvey has said, towards the "foregrounding of questions as to how radically different realities may coexist, collide, and interpenetrate" (Harvey 1990, 41). This is as true of the study of Ant as it is of anything else in this our present condition of postmodernity.

Recall that in "The Author of the Acacia Seeds" Le Guin skillfully transliterated four Ant passages written in touch-gland exudation on 31 acacia seeds (Le Guin, 3). From this she deduced that the ant-author was a wingless neuter-female worker, yearning, hopelessly, to be a winged male, free to fly off and found a new colony. Since dialects of Ant employ only the third person singular and plural and the first person plural, there was no way, Le Guin said, to decide "whether the passage was intended to be an autobiography or a manifesto" (4). Here Le Guin was overly cautious, in my opinion. I would urge her to consider the following: what if the author of the Acacia Seeds was innovating in Ant, to the extent of writing simultaneously *both* an autobiography *and* a manifesto? One suggestion is that we have here, in Ant, the work of an ant precursor of Germaine Greer, an inspired anticipation of *The Female Eunuch* (1971).[1]

What is important for my present purposes is the following. In interpreting the Acacia seed texts as a series of direct utterances in Ant, Le Guin moved from linguistic analysis of grammar and syntax into the dimension of myth and narrative. The ant's story is coded as feminist revolt against patriarchal oppression, a revolt that ends with the tragic death of the protagonist. Here Le Guin, our founding mother, was sketching the rudiments of a thero-narratology. She succeeded admirably in the modernist attempt to unify the fragments on the acacia seeds.

Yet in succeeding, did she not also fail? Did she not impose a feminist meta-narrative on the acacia seeds, a story with an old-fashioned beginning, middle, and (dread closure) end? All too soon she found herself embroiled in the large question, "What is Art?" (Le Guin, 9). This in relation to the art of *plants* proved a task beyond even her considerable talent. As for geolinguistics—to be the first to read "the still less communicative, still more passive, wholly atemporal cold volcanic poetry of the rocks" (11)—however high her hopes, her ambition foundered on rocky reality.

I decided to forget the question, "What is art?" And Since then I have never looked back. What happened was this. I began my studies in Ant, but soon found myself constrained by its limitations. I longed for a language with a more expansive literature than one to be found inscribed on just 31 acacia seeds. Le Guin studied Dolphin and Penguin and made a worthy attempt at the language of plants and rocks, and her efforts along these lines got me thinking. What if there was a language that juxtaposed elements of animal, plant, and rock together? That would knock the socks off David Harvey and his *Condition of Postmodernity* (1990). That would really foreground the question of how radically different realities can co-exist, collide, and interpenetrate.

This is where I claim to stand on the shoulders of the giant Le Guin to see a little further, to make my own contribution. Here I stand. I cannot do otherwise. Le Guin briefly mentioned the cold volcanic poetry of the rocks. The choice of volcanic rock was, I believe, unfortunate, for these are inorganic rocks, rocks from the hot brutal places of the earth, rocks that are not going to be bothered with human-earth communication other than to dump another load of lava from the heights of a lofty mountain vent.

I chose a softer, more empathic rock, a rock with feeling, sensitivity, and warmth. I chose to explore the language of corals.

Corals are the reef builders, a veritable collision in one organism of animal, plant, *and* rock. The coral body is a simple cylinder of tissue fringed by stinging tentacles, a veritable *vagina dentata* for its plankton prey. The mouth serves also, economically, as the anus (a matter that provides much Freudian grist to the thero-psychoanalyst's mill). Floating round the small polyp body are minute *plants*, algae called zooxanthellae. These give the polyp animal both its color and, through photosynthesis, its oxygen. Finally, the third element in the coral body is the rocky white calcareous exo-skeleton. Polyps are genetically identical clones, modular units of tissue and rock in constant communication. The coral body is the paradigmatic case of how radically different realities can co-exist, collide, and interpenetrate. Slippery, permeable, indefinable, corals stand in sharp contrast to ants, which, while part of a collective organization, are still solid, discrete, hard-shelled and essentially individualized.[2]

It is fair to say that since Le Guin's pioneering work, there has been a paradigm shift in understanding and writing the coral *body*. Photography has revealed (to humans) the fullness of coral bisexuality or modes of both sexual and asexual reproduction. Corals may be clones off the old coral block, primitive asexual creatures that bud and multiply *in situ*. But once a year, as has only been recently discovered, they get seriously mobile. Corals will work hard for months to produce eggs and packets of sperm. Then on the Great Barrier Reef on the sixth day after the first full moon in November, the polyps extrude their precious gamete packs. Floating to the surface of the water, these meet and fertilise as free-swimming, fast-wheeling *planulae*. Off they then go to distant lands and places. An example of how this story, till now, has been told, from *Sex on the Reef* (1993):

VIDEO	AUDIO
Packets of sperm and eggs squeeze from the coral body and float to the surface of the water, like stars in the night sky.	This is an evolutionary success story made possible by a remarkable reproductive strategy. Somewhere in their evolutionary past, corals struck a deal with zooxanthellae. Their partnering became a powerful evolutionary achievement. Between them, they built the reef.

So our conventional story goes. What to humans has been revealed only through painstaking observation and experiment, corals have known *in the coral body* for at least 240 million years. Stories humans tell about polyps, stories polyps tell about themselves—plenty of room here for fracture and collision in the disjuncture between colonial and postcolonial discourse. Collision, co-existence, inter-penetration, each fuels the cultural critic's deep desire.

Corals are the most skilled of all reef writers. Immersed as they are in water, their language is a fluid one, uniting elements of animal, plant, and rock. As they exist for the most part not as isolated individuals, but as modular units in colonies, their voice is a polyphonic *c(h)oral* voice.

Initially the secret of their writing was sought in polyp movement, but to no avail. It was only when attention was shifted from the visible world of polyp motion to the invisible world of chemical exchange that true understanding became possible. Just as the underwater camera revealed the beauty of the submarine worlds, so new mass-spectrometer tools of chemical analysis have revealed the central importance of oxygen. Yes, it is the zooxanthellae that control the emotional life of corals. Very small differences in the concentration of oxygen can give rise to headiness or despair. The zooxanthellae control oxygen like a drug.

The language of corals is, then, the language of oxygen, of a gaseous state of being. It is a series of texts written by air in water.

There will need to be some modification to reader-response theory in the light of gaseous texts. I make the following suggestions.

Take one reader, shake well, and suspend in ocean, feet first, snorkel firmly gripped in mouth. Lower until reader encounters coral text. Sense of radical otherness well-affirmed: reader breathes air while corals wave in water. Note undermining of claims to a privileged existence. Reader is scared half-crazy, wondering if air will keep coming down the pipe. Extraneous texts intrude. Is that a shark down below there in the shadows? When is a shark not a text? Or, as Derrida might have said had he thought to include the shark, there is just no way to perceive the watery world without that world being contaminated by language, e.g., the word "shark."

Perhaps the role of reader is determined by the text itself. Against the brute facts of its physical cloned existence, the polyp poses its idiosyncratic self. Here it is, the polyp self, a clone amongst clones, yet solitary with it. It is divided, yet a conglomerate: a free individual, yet bound by force of exo-skeletal circumstance. The reader reads and exits, leaving the text unchanged. No dissolution of readerly identity here.

It could be otherwise. Subversive coral texts undermine attempts at mastery. The gaseous text is read as fundamentally incomplete, with solidity and fluidity an additional construction of the act of reading. Reading the reef, e.g., in the transgressive act of fishing with dynamite, will not leave the coral text unaltered. The text will be remade, albeit as dead white chunks floating belly-up. In tracing the dissolution or dispersal of the text's identity, the reader makes the text, and the text makes the reader.[3]

Texts
C(h)oral Songs 1

Texts 1-13

Gold days of sea and summer. Enemy invades. Age of Ice. Cold war on corals. *Blurp blurp blurp*. Earth swings hot. Sea levels rise. Hot war on corals. Down with the Age of Ice. *Bad air in, good air out, blurp blibble blub*. Peace on our terms. Down with the Age of Heat. Peace will be on our terms. *Blip plip*. Power to the polyps!

Polyps blobby jellies suck. Power to the plants.

Texts 14-22

Where feel it? In the mouth-gut gut-mouth. A tingling of the tentacles, a lightness in the coelom. Ripeness is all. Egg package ripe. Sperm package ripe. The moon is full. November, month of summer madness. It. It happens. It. Release. Plop. Glop. Ahhhoohhh Yes! Oh yes! Yes!

Blobby jelly ploppy polyps suck. Yes yes yes yes.

Texts 23-29

Singing the zooxanthellae blues. Be pink? Be green? Be yellow? Be blue? Take bad gas in. Let good gas out. Busy, busy, busy. Who are the pretty algae then? In the full light of day, what shall our color be?

Zoox are so trivial.

Texts 30-31

Rock pound rock tight rock fit rock swell rock is. Rock is rock. Hit rock. Waves hit rock. Sand hits rock. Storm hits rock. Hit slap pound pummel slap strike crash rap punch. Water swells, swishes through. Polyps tickle. Zoox zoom.

C(h)oral Songs 2
Song Without End

Polyp leaves stony calcareous home and bails out, plopping flopping off into the water. Little tentacles clasped tight to small jelly chest, leaving being its extended clone family, taking off alone, looking for new free space to sit and collect about itself its new skeletal excrescence of lime, its new shell, new home, a clone colony of its own. Swishing, wishing wobbly/wobbly bailed out polyp, lonely, vulnerable, seeks new home space to move to spread its polyp wings, create a new home in far off watery rock-free places. Bail out/wobbly time. Not all things are rocky fixed. Polyps lighter than rock, heavier than water, squeeze through the interstices, bail out when squeezed too tightly to the neighbors, home no longer Home Sweet Home, too tight a squeeze. Seeking new home/home new skeletons. Old ones don't fit right any more. Old ones fixed and settled in their ways. Polyps depart on long and perilous voyage.

As you can see, where Le Guin tells a tragic tale of only one single protagonist with a fatal flaw, *C(h)oral Songs 1* and *2* allow for multiple voices. With the ant story, the message may live on, but the messenger dies in the attempt. Le Guin's protagonist was an ant whose fatal flaw was a tragic sense of her own uniqueness. Poor fatally flawed little creature, doomed to fail.

Earlier I suggested that the author of the Acacia Seed texts might be an ant-analogue of Germaine Greer. I would like to offer *C(h)oral Songs* in variegated, diffuse and contradictory voices à la Cixous/Kristeva/Irigaray. Feminism, though, of the Cixous/Kristeva/Irigaray variety is a lost cause on corals, which care not a whit for sexual difference. Male, female, they mix and match, here extruding sperm, there extruding eggs, elsewhere the egg-sperm packet, neatly wrapped. Coral identity is fissured, doubled, uncannily so, easily inhabited by others, zooxanthellae. The texts prompt us to ask, what is the essential coral, if it is doubled, tripled, cloned to near infinity, within itself?

Coral presents itself as indifferent to writing, indeed, without necessary arms or fingers for the task. As the Australian cultural critic McKenzie Wark might have said, if he'd thought about corals, theirs is a virtual language:

> That virtual side of language is its endless resources of sensation, of particular qualities it can express… Moments when, through the opaque sheet of language, we sense bodies moving, pulsating, mutating, just below the surface. The postmodern moment calls for those qualities of language as the resources necessary for making sense of the peculiarly novel and complex experiences of now, after the revolution has not come. (Wark 1997, 109)

(The corals have news for Wark. The revolution has not come, *yet*. They are working on it. Watch this space.)

Sometimes you hear it said of corals, that theirs is a rags to riches tale in which a poor little life form makes good, and through annual mass spawning achieves its ambitions for global expansion—indeed, to the point of dominion over the warm, shallow, tropical seas. The story is told so that humans, too, might take heart and learn what they might achieve through their own collective efforts and struggle. That is our story of them, but not their story of themselves. More research is called for. What are the words so that invertebrates may speak? What are some of the less-grand narratives that provide the silenced with voices?

The field is so vast, so new.

References

Harvey, David, *The Condition of Postmodernity. An Enquiry into the Origins of Cultural Change.* Cambridge: Blackwell, 1990.

Bennet, Andrew, and Royle, Nicholas. *An Introduction to Literature, Criticism and Theory. Key Critical Concepts.* London, Prentice Hall, 1995.

Greer, Germaine, *The Female Eunuch.* New York: McGraw Hill Book Company, 1971.

Le Guin, Ursula K. "The Author of the Acacia Seeds and Other Extracts from the Journal of The Association of Therolinguistics," *The Compass Rose.* London: Gollancz, 1983: 3-11.

Sex on the Reef. Videorecording, Janine Hadley and Russell Kelley, Coral Sea Imagery and Television New Zealand Natural History Unit Co-production, 1993.

Wark, McKenzie, *The Virtual Republic.* Melbourne: Allen and Unwin, 1997.

Notes

1. Or it may be that, just as Indo-European is a language extrapolated backwards from its present traces, so the grand meta-narrative of Ant was unconsciously extrapolated backwards from *The Female Eunuch.* This topic I leave for future scholars in the comparative, cross-species study of language, archaeology, and myth.

2. I am indebted to Brian Attebury for this insight.

3. See Andrew Bennet and Nicholas Royle, pp. 9-18, for a pre-coralline summary of reader-response theory.

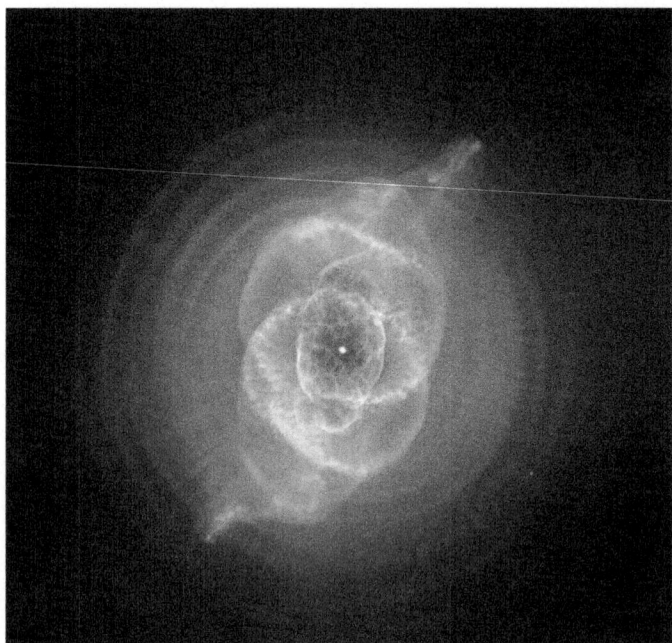

Bubbles in the
Cosmic Saucepan

I've heard that Europe will be vanquished in the next 10,000 years. It will not be the next world war or bombs that will ultimately destroy London, Paris, Rome, but the ice, which will spread southward from the Pole and cover the land. The sea level will fall, and Atlantis may rise from the waters, a possible place of refuge for the Swiss bankers and the army generals essential for the restoration of civilization once the ice retreats.

I've also heard that the hole in the ozone layer above Tasmania is growing bigger and that ultraviolet light will flood the earth, causing cancer in those who go out in the midday sun. Gases from the combustion of fossil fuels will rise to the upper layers of the air, raising the temperature a degree or two, melting the ice, causing the sea level to rise, flooding part of Melbourne, and heralding the beginnings of the next interglacial era.

With the waters destined either to rise or fall, migration to a mountain in Hawaii seems the answer.

Here we are, at just one transitional stage among many, between one stage of equilibrium and the next, between a state in which the human race has flourished and the next stage in which many of the oxygen-breathing species may prove redundant, and who knows what will emerge as the new dominant life form.

They'll soon get used to it, our descendents, living on the edges of either the swamps or the ice, scurrying under the feet of larger, more dominant forms of life, cane toads, or penguins, as once small rat-like creatures scurried under the clumping feet of the dinosaurs.

Summer, winter—the earth turns round the sun. Day, night—the earth spins on its axis. Or the starry sky above spins round. It's all relative.

Twenty thousand years ago glaciers pushed down from the mountains, and the wind roared round the fortieth parallel. The seas did not totally freeze, though rippling icy platforms spread out from the land far into the ocean, and large tabular icebergs floated by in the icy sea. The shoreline sloped under the ice to the water below, the seals chased the Adelie penguins, the whales filtered krill through their wide open mouths, and plankton followed the flow lines in the icy oceans. Bass Straight was a green and grassy plain. People walked from Victoria to Tasmania for the summer and camped on the edge of the ice, hunting the red-necked wallabies for their skins, searching in the caves for fatty, furry moths.

In ten thousand year's time from now, family life will be very different, though it need not be an inevitable decline into savagery as the ice descends, the power supply fails, and the demand for scarce resources more than usually outstrips supply. The human species will probably survive, though clad in kangaroo skins sewn with needles made from the teeth of bandicoots. Camels will make a come-back, and the wallaroos, and we shall all be hunter-gatherers again, in tune with the new environment if we are to survive, or totally at odds with it—in which case we quite possibly will not.

There will still be food when the next Ice Age comes and half the earth freezes and photosynthesis occurs for the same short time in the southern hemisphere as it does in the north. It should take six weeks to walk from Melbourne to the rim of the ice, six weeks to get back, and six weeks to summer over where the glaciers crash down from the mountains and the moths and the red-necked wallabies roam.

Families will gather once more around camp-fire middens. The children will learn how to haft stone axes with beeswax. Women will soften kangaroo tendons with their teeth, as they did in the old days. As will the men, for at least they will know more about fair shares with the division of labor between male and female and details about how teeth are formed and the beneficial (or not so beneficial) effects of fluoride on tooth enamel.

We shall not go unprepared into the next Ice Age as were the people who met with the last one. Everything is for the best in the best of all possible worlds, said Voltaire's Candide, until he knew better. And this takes his argument one step further into the new era. Everything is for the best in a world in which the cycles of nitrogen and carbon and hydrogen are once more operating smoothly through the realms of the animal and mineral and vegetable.

Or, it may be that the Greenhouse warming of the earth will come before the next Ice Age. As the waters of Sydney Harbor rise around the waterfront at Tooronga Park, the zoo will empty its stocks to the central desert, and okapi shall graze where now the lizards dwell. Hotter, cooler, who can tell?

There will come a time with cane toads born to rule, if only for the next few thousand million years. Who are human beings to object to another highly successful life form, just because it hops along on all fours and can't talk yet, or because it's an ugly yellowish green with poison glands under its wart-encrusted ears and a record of killing any animal up to twice its size. What if its sexual habits verge on the quite disgusting, with on occasion a preference for a partner well and truly dead and decayed past putrefaction into desiccation? That's what sexual preference is all about: one man's putrescent cane toad being another cane toad's delight. Sexual preference, too, must be subject to the changing conditions of life.

It may be that measurements taken over a mere one hundred years can tell something, but not enough. The last 10,000 years may show an upward trend of destruction, but what then? Change happens: take the very long-term view, and there are always variations, so that present fluctuations in the seasons are as nothing compared with the changes wrought by the coming and going of the glaciers, with their great sheets of glittering reflective ice.

Opportunistic, entrepreneurial, the earth folds all to its capacious breast. What matters is the whole, more than the sum of its parts. The parts are interchangeable, providing they are many.

We are but bubbles in the cosmic saucepan.

The system can accommodate a lot of variation, but one day, no longer. It packs it in. It loses its amazing elasticity, quite suddenly, and slips sideways into a new way of being, overcome by forces that can no longer be accommodated. Its equilibrium has been punctuated, *status quo* upset, and it is the system, after all. It has the upper hand, though it has chosen up till now to exercise its control in ways that are relatively benign.

Far above the earth and beyond, the universe is in the state of becoming. Quarks add to quarks, mesons to pions, neutrons to protons, and quite ordinary matter moves from the relatively simple to the absolutely complex. Nothing to begin with—then the Big Bang. And primitive hydrogen is formed, and more complex elements in their turn; until the interstellar gases condense, and the stars shine in the sky, and nucleosynthesis deep inside the outer glow forms elements more complex still, and new stars are born, collapse, and die, and in exploding carry their debris into the remoter reaches of the ever-expanding cosmos.

One day, nothing; then matter, in all its pure simplicity of form. Matter becomes more complex, and aspires to higher and higher degrees of organization. Throw ice into some water and heat it. The molecules will vibrate faster and faster, caught up in the fixed arrangements they bear to each other, but as they speed up certain fixed limits will be exceeded, and change will be fast, sudden, and discontinuous. Ice enters the new realm of water, just as a rope that has been stretched to its limit breaks to form something similar, but different: two pieces of rope.

The amoeba has little consciousness of self. It knows only to turn to light and away from darkness. The universe has up till now had much the same reflex action to its activities. Once a higher level of organization is reached, there may well emerge a cosmic consciousness as a new factor to be taken into account in everyday life.

One day we shall all be going about our business. The next day there will be the voice of the aware cosmos booming in our ears, telling us what it thinks it is, and where it thinks it is going. Not too worried about the sentient forms of lower life that happen to be wriggling round its interstices. The cosmic consciousness, when it comes, will probably be as concerned about us as we are about the buzzing fly or the self-important gnat.

Information overload. The voices on the radio are the background noise against which lives are lived, personal decisions are taken, interpersonal crises are daily rehearsed. The voices on the radio report what is happening, and the voices go out into the void.

What are words, but wave motion in the air, tripping out in all directions from a central point of origin. What are words but electronic messages along telecommunication channels. Electrons flow, air molecules vibrate, making a series of not-so-random disturbances in the information field. Billions of molecules dance to new tunes.

I hear the voices and I try to understand. Today: neatness and order. Tomorrow: chaos. That is the nature of the world. We are on the edge of the abyss, about to fall off the edge of the flat earth, to be sucked into the black hole by who knows what, some cosmic vacuum cleaner perhaps. Who knows whose finger is on the button, ready to tidy up this earthly mess.

Better not to know.

Things when they change will change unpredictably. Look at the lesson of the dinosaurs for proof that chance and change and perhaps a sideswipe from a passing comet will tip the balance of nature into an entirely new way of being. One day everyone will be going about their business, expecting the sun to rise tomorrow. Then the next day, it won't happen. Everyone will be surprised and annoyed—and doubtless, like the dinosaurs, dead within days.

Deep in the jungle the butterfly beats its wings, and the changes it creates help generate a tornado that flattens houses half a world away.

What if, though. What if as the next stage of human evolution, a sixth sense emerges into human awareness. What if by some means people grow into a fuller sense of the electrical world around them, just as they have grown into a partial awareness of some manifestations of it, in light and sound?

What if, one day, as the world tips sideways into a new way of being, all the electricity that is leaking from the power lines and the transformers, the television towers and the satellite dishes, what if it should turn the human body electric and change the course of evolution? Today's wild idea may be tomorrow's accepted fact. Or today's lunatic theory may be tomorrow's lunatic theory, but who will know before tomorrow comes?

One day, some people will develop an electric sense. They will know what it is, in the way everyone knows the wind is blowing in their face or feels the water flowing over their skin. First one person will sense it, and then another, and such is the power of a new insight, a new habit of life, such is the capacity of the human mind to adapt, to understand, that knowledge will quickly transmit itself across the globe, even into remote villages where pollution of the environment with electronic radiation has never been much of a problem. All over the world the new knowledge will soon replace the old.

Of course, people will deny it, at first. Then they'll get used to it and accept it. Accept that this is the way things happen. One day, it will be forgotten that once things were different. That before the electrical machines came, things were simpler, somehow.

We shall see people in refrigerator shops, electric passion throbbing through their veins, their hair stiff with static. Shameless with it, in love with their iPods and their pop-up toasters. A new electric love, a love that transcends the old distinctions, drawing on a deeper kind of affinity, working at the level of the electrons, the quarks even, plugging into the electrical heartbeat at the center of creation. The private world of each individual person will link and merge into some kind of shared public electromagnetic world.

The earth will still spin round. Lines of force will sweep down from the far reaches of the cosmos, buffeted by the solar winds, dancing with the green light of the Aurora, looping through the magnetosphere, traveling deep down into the earth. Along the way waves of electric love will pass their message through various organic nervous systems, deep down into the neurons, sparking the higher levels of consciousness, uniting all in the forces of creation.

The earth will make a sideways slip, and things will be forever different. People will adapt themselves quite well to the change, and only occasionally, in the middle of the night, will someone sit up and say, "Didn't things once used to be different?"

The notion will soon be lost in the confusion of other night thoughts and will not survive into the waking day.

In Tribulation and with Jubilee: On Pilgrimage with Bridie King

First email
Subject: Roadtrip with Bridie
From: R.Love@headspace.edu.au
To: dear friends and all

I am writing and cc'ing this letter to tell you about my travels so far.

I am on the road to New Orleans with my cousin Bridie King. For those of you out of the loop, I've been living in the USA for the past couple of months, in St. Louis, and my cousin Bridie, who lives in Sydney, has arrived for a flying visit. Bridie is a Sydney rhythm-and-blues legend. She's the charismatic bandleader and wild pianist of Bridie and the Boogie Kings. Together, we're on a road trip to New Orleans. Bridie can't drive. I can. We're a team. I'm driving Miss Bridie. Miss Bridie, in turn, is showing me her world.

Bridie is on a pilgrimage. She is going to the source of her music. She has a minidisk recorder in hand, and she is unstoppable.

Bridie arrived in St. Louis on Tuesday, October 5, on time at 7.19 pm, having had a comfortable flight from Australia on a half-empty United Airlines flight. Those of you who have flown United on the long-haul Sydney-San Francisco leg will know this was the first miraculous event of the pilgrimage.

As we got out of our rented car at the back of my house in St. Louis, we heard a live band in the distance, from the direction of Forest Park. We just had to go. We drove to the park while Bridie wrestled a disk into her recorder in the dark, cellophane rustling, disk inserted every wrong way till the right way. It turned out to be the Skipdaddies playing a gig at the free summer concerts at the Missouri History Museum. It was getting cold, and the audience was starting to leave as we arrived. Bridie mooched around and started chatting to the guy running the electronic control thingie. Despite signs forbidding electronic recording, she got him talking on tape about the music scene in St. Louis, to a Skipdaddies original backing.

Early Wednesday we started on our way, detouring unintentionally through some of St. Louis's classy gated communities. I had never driven in the USA before, and it took a few wrong turns to find the local supermarket for our road trip munchies.

On the way south we skirted Memphis, as we planned to visit Graceland on the return trip. It was obvious from the plethora of Graceland road signs we'd have no trouble finding it. In our first major experience of freeway interchanges, we managed, miraculously, to go around Memphis and emerge on the other side, still on Interstate 55, and still alive. Pleased with ourselves and stunned by the experience, we pulled into the next diner we saw. I am skipping non-music detail, though I must say that Bridie is choosing the places to stop for a break, and our first coffee stop had been at a Skinnies Diner earlier in the day, where Bridie started chatting to people about how she's never been in a diner before and is on a pilgrimage.

We sat at the bar of the Memphis diner, and Bridie began ordering. Bridie ordering coffee is a class act. She told the waitress that we were sorry all we wanted was a coffee because we'd eaten earlier at another diner and these diners were amazing and she'd just come from Australia and this was her second day in the USA.

"What brings you to Memphis?" the waitress asked.

Bridie's eyes glowed. "I just love Elvis."

The waitress gave Bridie an odd, evaluative look. "You just love Elvis, huh?"

"I just love Elvis."

"Want to meet his cousin?"

Turned out the waitress was married to Elvis' cousin, and he was in the diner. The next minute we were chatting to Butch, kin to Elvis, as he explained the relationship in a melodious speech linking his Mammy's Mam to Elvis's family. Bridie didn't have the minidisk working at that moment so the exact relationship wasn't caught on disk. Butch sized up Bridie, letting her know from the start he didn't hold with any kind of hysterical Elvis worship. He didn't visit the grave. He just liked to remember Elvis as he once was, without the posthumous fuss.

Bridie's technique is part wild enthusiasm, part prodigious knowledge of music. I was initially skeptical. We go into a diner outside Memphis and Bridie meets Elvis's second cousin, oh yeah. But my misgivings were soon quelled. Butch too is a muso and had played in Sydney, and Bridie coaxed him to talk about his work and the music he played with Elvis. We went into the car-park, and Butch talked with Bridie on the minidisk, something he initially refused to do because he didn't want to give interviews without knowing how they would be used. Before we parted forever, in the car-park, Bridie gave Butch a big hug and a copy of her CD *My Blues*.

The first day was not yet over. We planned to spend the night in Oxford, Mississippi. We drove in just as it was getting dark and set out for Ole Miss (the University of Mississippi). We drove in, parked near the old observatory, and walked around. Bridie had the vague intention of searching out the Center for Southern Culture, but we didn't know where it was, and we got side-tracked. Outside the student union, a girl with a guitar was singing a mournful song about love lost and found again. We stopped, Bridie chatted with her, and out came the minidisk for another interview and a recording. It was a balmy southern evening. We were on the steps of a university notorious in the history of the Civil Rights Movement for the violence that accompanied the enrollment of James Meredith, its first black student, in September 1962. Forty plus years later, who'd have guessed it. Two boys walked over to see what was happening, and Bridie recorded the song. Black students, white students, happy together, in their music.

Next day we drove cross-country to Clarkesdale, to the Delta Blues Museum. Bridie was tossing up about Clarkesdale and whether we might skip it, but it was only eighty miles away, and it was a lovely day, so we went. Once more, it was a case of Bridie's luck. At Clarkesdale, we stopped off at the Cat Head, Delta Blues and Folk Art shop, where Bridie learned that the annual King Biscuit Blues Festival was about to start in Helena, Arkansas, some forty miles up the road. It was too good to miss. We decided we'd drive up to Helena and check it out. But where would we stay? Accommodation might be tight at a festival billed as the World's Largest Free Blues Festival, which it probably is. Bridie started asking round Cat Head about accommodations. Bridie's luck again: Frank (Rat) Ratcliffe, the proprietor of the Clarkesdale Riverside Hotel, happened by and Bridie met him. The two of them hit it off, and we found our beds for the night.

The Riverside Hotel is billed as "the home of the Delta Blues" and has every right to its claim. It's on the bank of the Sunflower River, on the wrong side of the Clarkesdale tracks. The hotel was once the black hospital where the singer Bessie Smith was taken in 1937, having earlier been refused admission to the whites-only hospital. She was admitted dead on arrival, in a situation where she might have survived had help been given earlier. At the Riverside Hotel, you can sleep in Bessie Smith's room, and there's a picture of Bessie

Smith on the wall. Bridie sat on the bed and recorded her emotions on minidisk.

We booked in for a night in a room that has seen a great many previous visitors, but it was fine. It was for music. John F Kennedy Jr had stayed at the hotel, and his picture was on the wall, though what impressed Bridie more was the news that Ike Turner had recorded in the basement.

We next stopped at the Clarkesdale Information Center, where we went to email our New Orleans hosts about our change of plans. I stayed in the car, studying the road maps, while Bridie went inside. She tried to send her email, failed, came out and got me. I showed both Bridie and Shona from the center how to get onto email (I have some areas of knowledge), and both were mightily impressed. Bridie sent her email, noticed a piano in the corner, asked if she could play, and before much time had passed Shona was singing gospel and Bridie was playing for her. Fortunately nobody came in for information, though I expect if anyone had dropped by, they would have joined in and sung along.

We spent the rest of the day at the festival in Helena, a town that seemed, on first tourist glance, to be even more "poor south" than Clarkesdale. A three-story façade of a burned-out shop stands in the main street facing the festival site, an object of curiosity only to tourists. The locals no longer notice. We found a place to sit on the grassy levee just by the old railway tracks. The Mississippi flowed by on the other side of the levee, and the cement works down by the river belted dust over everyone. Bridie ate some barbecue cooked in a device that resembled a moonshine still and could have well been one once. Later, she felt jetlagged and took a nap in a quiet corner of the nearby Delta Museum, her head resting on a small bale of cotton in the caboose of an old river steamer.

When Bridie swung into action again, she really got going. In spite of signs saying no recording devices, she interviewed the people we sat next to on the levee about the music they liked. The interviewees included, variously, the security guard at the local Isle of Capri casino out with his wife and energetic small boy for a day at the music, a dapper photographer, elegant in black bowler hat and flashy tie, and, later, Fonzie and his wife Jirell of Fonzie's Bar, a red neon-lit juke bar that Bridie just loved. It was mostly empty though, that night, because everyone was outdoors, down by the Mississippi.

Late at night we drove back to Clarkesdale over dark country roads where the cell phone was way out of range, and I started to wonder whether the car rental insurance covered us for the back-blocks of Arkansas.

I have to say it was an uncomfortable night we spent at the Riverside Hotel in Clarkesdale, largely because of the plastic undersheets thoughtfully provided by the management for those with a bladder problem or too much to drink.

After fond farewells to Frank, where Bridie has made yet another friend for life, we set out for New Orleans. The first stop was Jackson, Mississippi, where Bridie wanted to find a famous recording studio, Malaco. All she had was the name of the studio—no address, no introduction. We drove into Jackson, parked at the first car-park we saw, and started out. We'd forgotten about paying for parking, but the car-park attendant came out of his shed and asked for $5. It was raining. Bridie had no umbrella. The attendant's shed looking inviting. So Bridie got him talking about what music he liked, and half an hour later we had another tape, of Lamarr tuning to his favorite Jackson radio stations, his faves being traditional jazz and neo-gospel. Bridie quizzed him some more about neo-gospel and where we might go to hear it. Lamarr rang his friend, the gospel singer Miss Smith, who told him more about Malaco studio, and we were given directions to Bebop records where Bridie could go first in order to get an introduction to the studio.

As Bridie was chatting to Lamarr and recording him, the security guy drove up, and various other people came in to pay for parking. Bridie got the security guard (gun on hip) talking about what he liked in country music, though she has a principle of only taping black people, and he was not only white, he didn't know much about country music either. It was, however, a wise thing to do. Later we followed Lamarr's excellent directions to Bebop Records where Bridie chatted to the guy at the ticket-tek counter while the people in line behind us tried to buy tickets to things, and with a bit of ringing around, he organized a jam session in Jackson the next Tuesday night with the locals at the studio. We then drove to the studio to see where it was. Bridie was tired by this time and didn't go in. This was most uncharacteristic.

The rest of the day? The drive into New Orleans took us across miles of causeway over the bayou, at dusk, then at rush hour in the rain into New Orleans along a twenty-lane freeway, with Bridie on the cell-phone getting navigation instructions from her friends in New Orleans and relaying them to me. Bridie is not a driver and was also chatting about other things. We made it. What will today bring?

Cheers

Rosaleen

Second Email
From: R.Love@headspac.edu.au
Subject: Time of Tribulation
To: all

Dear Family and friends (those still reading after my first email re Bridie and our travels),

The rain we encountered on driving into New Orleans on October 8 turned into a Force Three storm the next morning, and all we could do was sit inside and watch the rain come down. I am glad I got to see New Orleans while it is still there. One day, and soon-ish, water will cover it.

It will no doubt not surprise you to learn that after a magnificent beginning to our travels, the pilgrimage foundered, if only temporarily. The dark night of the soul descended upon Bridie in the form of a particu-larly nasty virus. It did not help in the slightest that people had helpfully said, before she set out, oh everyone gets sick on planes. Bridie did not believe them, but even the power of her disbelief did not affect the course of this virus, which was vicious and brought Bridie up as still as she gets. Did I mention that in addition to her pilgrimage, Bridie is completing a subject in her Master's degree in music from Sydney University, and on the trip she had also to write some more of her research proposal? Bridie got sick in New Orleans, but she soldiered on regardless, and at least some of the research proposal got written.

We both agreed (later in the calmer light of after-illness) that a pilgrimage has to encounter obstacles; otherwise it's not a real pilgrimage, just too good a time. New Orleans, the anticipated highlight, was a near washout for Bridie. She didn't get to hear Zydeco music (Cajun Blues) at a local festival, part of which may well have been washed out by the rain anyway, and she didn't get to hear the gospel singing at the Ebenezer Missionary Baptist Church on Sunday.

A couple of really nice things did happen despite all. On Saturday afternoon her friends Julia and Dan took her to the Spotted Cat, a jazz bar in Frenchmen Street. It's at the edge of the French Quarter, a few streets outside, and away from the main tourist drag of Bourbon Street, a street that Dan said was a rip-off re the price of drinks. On Saturday afternoon, the Spotted Cat has the piano free to whoever convinces the management they can play, and Bridie did this, no worries. Despite the ever-strengthening virus, Bridie played a few pieces, including some boogie-woogie, and got a couple of bar regulars to sing along with her (was it to Down by the River?) in that marvelous way she has of including everyone in her music.

According to bar legend, the honky-tonk piano at the Spotted Cat once belonged to James Booker, one of Bridie's idols, but its provenance, when Bridie asked for evidence, was a wee bit hazy. Perhaps it was once his. Perhaps not. Somebody once broke the piano bench, and the discovery was made then. Perhaps it was James Booker's piano bench? Certainly, he must at least have played the piano. The manager, Slim, said they had a history of the piano written up somewhere. Bridie was pleased no matter what.

Everyone at the Spotted Cat loved Bridie, to shouts of "She's got soul!" and "Awesome!"

Two guys said: "All day we were asking, where's the good Music, and here it is. We went to the Information Center, and they said here. And now we're going back to the Information Center and tell them that we found it."

I bet if Bridie gets back to the USA, she could get a professional gig, no worries. We stayed on to hear the next act, a trio led by the deadpan Chaz. His washboard came customized with two former fruit tins and a wooden block for extra percussive effects, with a shop-bell to the side. Veritably, Chaz was playing the Stradivarius of the washboard. He dinged his shop-bell with panache. His songs were of a joyous melancholy persuasion. He's been in trouble all his life, he's met the wrong kind of woman, but if all night long we sing this song, if you get this song, you can't go wrong. You see a woman down Bourbon Street, he said, better have a good look, because it could be the wrong kind of woman. We've warned. Now we know.

We went out to eat, then caught a couple of acts at the Blue Nile opposite while Bridie felt worse and worse but kept going nonetheless. She held out for Bill Summers and wild Afro-Cuban jazz and was pleased at the time, but sorry the next day.

Monday morning Bridie really crashed, but managed a trip that night to Donna's Bar, where the Bob French band has been playing for years, ever since the time of one of the greats—was it Louis Armstrong?—with, at the beginning, Bob French Senior in charge, while now it's Bob French Junior. Bridie chatted to the pianist and learned that one of her pianist heroes, Alan Toussaint, had been to the bar the previous three Fridays. He was someone she'd hoped to meet, and it might have happened, except for the virus. It was a very near miss. One day, he'll be there again, and so will she, let's hope. We'd been warned when we went to Donna's to keep to the French Quarter and not to cross Rampart Street to the north. But there was no danger of that. The other side of the street was pitch dark, except for the Luna-Park-style illuminations of the gates to the Louis Armstrong Park. The name of the park was picked out in neon lights, with, underneath, the face of a clown missing half its neon-lit smile. I have never seen anything more sinister in my life.

The next day, we gave in to illness and packed up to go back to St. Louis. By the time we reached Memphis, Bridie was starting to feel better, and we stopped off at Graceland for an early-morning visit to the Elvis shrine. It was fun.

Along the way, as Bridie flipped the car radio dial, we experienced a hallelujah moment, a portent of what was yet to come. Bridie tuned into a gospel radio station. The guy sang "Hallelujah!" and it sounded pretty impressive to me. The girl said, "That's not how you sing that hallelujah!" and she belted out a joyous hallelujah melisma that took at least a couple of minutes to sing from beginning to end. Her hallelujah was way longer than his. The gospel station bills itself as Hallelujah Radio.

We got back to St. Louis, Bridie recovered, and we set off again for Memphis. From this point on, the focus of the pilgrimage changed. We went in search of neo-gospel, and we found it.

To be concluded next time.

Third Email
Subject: Jubilee
From: R.Love@headspace.edu.au
To: dear friends and all

Bridie decided on Friday, October 15, that we'd return to Memphis. She was starting to feel somewhat better, and she'd had two good days back at St. Louis working on the thesis proposal and sleeping the virus off, and Memphis is only five hours drive down the road from St. Louis. Only five hours? I was getting a bit blasé about driving in the USA. Bridie only had a few days left before her return flight to Sydney.

Bridie wanted to get to some recording studios in Memphis and also to a gospel concert we'd heard advertised on the radio on the previous trip. She'd caught a song by one group participating and its lead singer, John P Kee, and when she first heard him, she was mightily impressed. All we had was his name from the radio program, and at first we had the wrong name. Sounded to us like John P King. (We were both genetically pre-disposed to hear the word King for Kee, I expect, Bridie being the daughter of Ulick King and me the daughter of his brother Oliver King.) It didn't matter. We started at Stax Studios, with the all-day fund-raiser we'd also heard advertised on radio, a sing-in and play-in with students from the Stax Studio music school, broadcast by the gospel radio station. Our plan was to drop by, see what was happening, and ask around about the gospel concert.

By the time we left Stax Studios, we had the place— Mt. Sinai Missionary Baptist Church on Horn Lake Road—but not the street number. We decided to drive out to find the church, find what time it started, then come back to the motel, get changed, eat, etc., and return.

But first, Bridie realized she'd left her best shoes back in St. Louis, and it wouldn't do at all, both for church on Saturday night and for the gospel church service she wanted to go to on Sunday at Al Green's Full Gospel Tabernacle. (Before he came to his calling at the church, Al Green was a famed R&B singer leading the average jazz muso's life. Then, after his girlfriend threw a bowl of hot grits on him, burned him badly, felt remorse, and killed herself, he saw the light, repented of his sins, and came back to the church. I think that's the story, or part of it.)

Bridie needed shoes. And here's her chance. We passed a garage sale in someone's front yard. Bridie was dead serious about those shoes. I'd have gone in runners. We missed one garage sale through my incredulity, so we had to stop at the next one we saw. I dropped Bridie off and found somewhere to park. By the time I'd caught up with Bridie, she was engrossed in conversation with Deborah, whose sale it was, having discovered that Deborah had been the back-up singer for Al Green's last overseas tour.

Can this be possible, I asked myself yet again. Bridie has, quite by chance, met another marvelous musician. Deborah works at a local recording studio. Another great contact for Bridie. Bride gave Deborah her CD, and Deborah in return gave Bridie a pair of shoes, a fair trade, and they swapped business cards, phone numbers, addresses, etc, and I know Bridie will wear Deborah's shoes with great pleasure, and keep in touch with her.

As we went driving off again, I got to thinking about Bridie's multiple talents, not only with music, but with people. She must look at the people she meets and know: here's a music lover, a musician. Or else, everyone we met on that trip had music in their bones, and all it needed was someone like Bridie who can talk about the music they love and draw them out. There were a couple of young men she didn't talk to, standing as they were at a street corner in the middle of the day, and Bridie did query, Crack dealers? as we passed, and for all I know, she was spot-on. But I expect, if we'd stopped, she would have asked them about their music come what may, and they'd have told her. At length. Possibly at gunpoint.

We had arrived in Memphis and found our motel earlier, at about 2 pm. It was now getting on for 5. We set off to find the Mt. Sinai Missionary Baptist Church, via another recording studio, the Royal or the Regal, which was closed, though Bridie took a photo. We found the Mt. Sinai church, way down a road out of Memphis, nearly out of Tennessee and into Mississippi.

Bridie really loved her time in Mississippi. I'm thinking of Bridie in front of one of the huge stacks of harvested cotton, like cotton haystacks, that were scattered through the fields at this time of the cotton harvest. I've got a photo. The stacks had cotton sheet protective coverlets on top of them, like tarps, and the stacks were often inscribed with spray-on paint slogans, usually political or religious. The stack in my photo says **VOTE KERRY FOR PRESIDENT OF IRAQ**. Bridie stands beside it, minidisk in hand, as if interviewing the cottonstack about its tastes in music. Red-neck country and western, perhaps?

Back to Mt. Sinai Missionary Baptist Church. What did we find when we got there? Shock, horror. What was this? The church car park was filling. It was 5.20, and the car park attendant told us the concert started at 6. Consternation. No time to return and clean up. No time to eat. Time to get parked, go in, and get a seat.

While I parked, Bridie got talking with the couple parking next to us, George and Nancy. Bridie told George she was worried that she hadn't got changed for church, but George assured her he was going just as he was, not dressed up at all, and we'd be fine. George invited us to come into the church with them, which was great as he correctly divined that Bridie wanted to sit up right close to the action, and he did, too. George and Nancy led us to the second row of the church, a place we'd have been too self-conscious to have taken ourselves, as we seemed to be the only white people in a crowd of five hundred or so. It was a bit too close to five huge amps for me, but I am a wimp that way. Those drummed hemi-demi-semiquavers, whatever, are still reverberating through my bones.

The jubilee concert ran for five and a half hours, non-stop from 6 till 11.30. Music just flowed over and through, professionally produced to a very high standard. First up was Shea Norman, who, from the piano, led a choir and the audience through a seemingly impromptu praise session that lasted forty minutes. Other groups included the quartet of preacher-singers from Arkansas, Eternal Light, a trio called Perfection, and Jeffery Williams and his choir, the Voices of Inspiration. The Voices of Inspiration moved in wild aerobic rhythm, various conductors stepping democratically out of then back into the choir and dancing as they beat the time.

Neo-gospel, Bridie explained to me, has a Stevie Wonder influence, with funk and rock. It's characterized by mass-choir effects, where traditional gospel is more quartets singing in harmony. In neo-gospel, large choirs often sing in unison while in the instrumental section the drum beat is hemi-demi-semiquavers, whatever, fast and furious. Various solo singers step out from the choir and improvise magnificent cadenza-like lines, then step back. It's exhilarating to watch, listen, and dance to, as lots of people did, either standing up in their seats or out the front. I couldn't pick up many words of the songs, which kind of defeated one part of the gospel message. Except, possibly, the words are often the same, and everyone else knows them. Two children sang a duet, Brandon aged 11 and Chardae aged 10, possibly brother and sister. They were brilliant.

The last act, John P Kee, turned out to be a disappointment. His songs were being recorded live, and things went wrong, and he behaved like a sulky Hollywood film star, which he may well also be. His session ended with a horrible act for children, mimed by Rufus, a person in a huge human puppet head who couldn't act, move, or sing, given he couldn't see past his huge puppet nose. Rufus merchandise was for sale afterwards. Enough said.

Occasionally between groups there'd be a bit of talk from the stage, with the pianist keeping up a continuo undercurrent, as speakers filled in the gaps between groups. One of the speaker/preachers, Kim from the gospel station in Memphis, exhorted us to praise our sponsors, and there was general praise for Holiday Inn from time to time, which I thought a bit odd, but everyone tolerated it gracefully. Hallelujah. Amen. (Later someone explained to me that Holiday Inn is special because it was for a time the only motel chain that didn't discriminate against blacks.) Wanda, a candidate for an education post in the upcoming elections, came up on stage and spoke with Kim, and after trading a few Biblical quotations, Wanda asked people to vote for her. (George and Nancy were most unimpressed with soliciting votes in church.)

John P Kee introduced the pastor, Gerald Rayborn, who, said John P Kee, was in a time of trouble. The pastor mentioned his troubles, which seemed indeed troubling. He's been found guilty of improperly engaging in interstate commerce over the burning down of the previous Mt. Sinai MB church, and he faces sentencing on November 19. He was quite philosophical about it all and said, if God has called him to preach in jail, he'll go to preach in jail. Later he broke away from the group on stage to answer a call on his mobile phone, which, given the circumstances, was understandable. His lawyer? Apparently arson wasn't really the main issue, being, it seems, admitted. It was the interstate commerce issue that did him in.

At the end of the evening, George and Nancy waited for us and insisted we follow their car in convoy so that we could find our motel. It was great of them. We'd have found it, eventually, but we were both exhausted by then. And very hungry.

OK, that's it. More happened, including Bridie's attendance at Al Green's church the next day, where Al Green himself wasn't present, but Al Greene Senior, his elderly father, was in fine fettle. Bridie didn't last out the full three hours of the service, leaving after only two (the wimp). We went to Sun Studios, and Bridie played the piano in the studio where Elvis was first discovered. We went to Beale Street. We saw the Memphis pyramid in the distance.

But emails should never be this long.

My last image is of Bridie dipping her toes in the Mississippi. It's hard to walk in the waters of the Mississippi, as there are lots of flood control levees that stop you getting down to the river, but she wanted to get her feet wet in the water. At the old French settlement of St. Genevieve, just off the road some sixty miles south of St. Louis, I found a road to the river. Bridie scrambled down the rocky banks and stood up in the strong current. I've got her caught in a photo, lifting her hands in praise just as she was shown how to in Al Green's tabernacle, where Al Greene Senior said, "Uncrook your arms." And there she is, arms uncrooked, reaching out in the gospel gesture of praise. She looks really happy.

Once Giants Roamed the Earth

The sea murmurs on the rocks. Last night, there was no murmur. There were no rocks. The thing was out there, lying there, and when it stirred, the waters moved up and over and under, and the thing was there, underneath, near the surface. It's gone today.

If Kai goes to the jetty and jumps into the water, he'll be in way over his head. The thing that came yesterday has gone away today.

It will come back.

Kai knows. He's heard this story before. It's a story from the old people.

They're here today, the government people, to talk to the old people about sea rights and land rights, but their talk is just hot air. Kai knows better. That mob, they own this land, from here to the horizon. Sea, land, doesn't matter. What's under the water, in the bay, it's land, right? Happens for now to be covered by sea.

For the moment.

Wasn't always like that, in the time before this time; won't always be like that, in the time to come. What is sea was once land; what is now land was once sea.

The gods walked on the earth. They came to a place they liked, and there they settled. They turned into land, the gods, and look, you can see, there, how across the bay, that island, a god lay down, and stretched out, and there you can see the curve of his back, and in those rocks you can see where he set down his fishing net. And that's his canoe: must've got wrecked, like, just a bit, and he said, No worries. I like it here, the bay, the sea-grasses, the mangroves. It's a good place. It's home.

Sea rights. That's what it's about. From these shores to the horizon, who owns what.

Last night, Kai stepped out. He walked out on the water. He's not going to tell them today, that mob from the government. They wouldn't know how to listen, so hung up on their rights are they, on their legal rights. Who owns what, from the shore to the horizon, and the land that's there, under the water? They reckon, no-one. Others know better.

Last night, when Kai walked on the water, the sea sloshed round his ankles. His feet gripped what lay beneath, firm enough to give him rubbery passage, though his toes had to dig down deep.

Kai was there, when the sea rose and flooded the jetty and swept the men away, and their dog.

It was the dog that saved the fishermen, that's for sure, Chippie, the old red mongrel who came to after the flood, and found himself standing on top of the ocean, far from shore, far enough, in a different enough place, to make an old dog yelp himself silly. They came to, the men, Kurt and Eddie, with Chippie howling, and lights from the shore beaming out, and the rescue party turning up, their boats impossible to launch on the rubbery sea until they, too, the rescuers, learned not to fear, but to step out on sea as on land, in the knowledge that what was under the water would sustain them for the duration. The rescuers came in the moonlight, over the sea, to where the three men flopped round on top of the water, there to save them, three Jonahs from the belly of the deep.

Old Wally was in a bad way, but Kurt and Eddie, they were big men, and they came to and gave Wally the kiss of life, that's what brought him back, as Chippie barked his head off, and Wally woke to curse his rescuers, but he's not too sorry, not today.

They took Wally off to the hospital, just to be sure. At the time, his story made no sense.

One of the Government men is back today, with something he wants the old people to look at. He's brought the drum from the museum and the museum people with their video cameras. They want the old people to tell the old stories. The old people are happy to oblige. They like the old stories, but better still, they like to turn the old stories into new stories.

The people gathered under the trees and passed the drum around carefully, whispering. On the rim of the drum they traced here the marks of the sun as it shimmers on calm noon water, there the glimmer of the full moon on the place where salt water meets fresh. The story is told in the marks. The story is told in the music. The story is told in the dance. Today there is no music, no dance. The story will be told, but not fully.

Kai's there, at the meeting place, with the old people, to help fill in the silence with words, to make the museum guys feel good about their meeting.

"You bang that drum," they murmured, the old people, one to another, "Trouble comes looking for you. Big time."

Kai was there, the go-between, the interpreter, to tell the museum guy that the drum was played on special occasions, to summon the creatures of the deep. Maika, they said, it's her drum, and Maika is from the old times. Maika, she traveled south with her mate, and as she traveled, she created all the land along the coast, and all the people, all the families, all the creatures of the shore.

Someone's given that drum a bash, they reckon, the old people. They whisper their agreement. That's what happened yesterday. Those fellas in the museum, they packed the drum to bring it up here, and some smart-arse played the fool and thumped it, and that's why it happened. The fishermen, and Chippie. That's the drum of Maika, who traveled down this coast and created the bays, the rocks, the headlands, the islands. She traveled south, and now she's on the move again. She's come here, and she's mad. That storm—her breath—made the clouds. That flood tide—her spirit—frothed the salt spray. That land under the sea, it's her resting place, a place for which they have a name and the government lot do not.

Maika is moving now. She's moving because she's heard about them fellas, she's heard about the new laws that say sea places are owned by everyone and no-one. Maika doesn't like that, so that is what she is saying, that is what all this means. Them fellas on the jetty last night, who were swept away into the water, they could have drowned. But they were saved—that time. Maika, she did that.

Not like she'll change her ways, not for the government people and their laws that are not her laws. Their laws will wash away in the salt and the spray.

The old folks, they knew. That night, last night, they weren't down by the sea, not like those men who got swept away. The old people stayed up high, on the cliffs, and made their fire. They looked out over the sea and the islands, and inland to the place where the fresh water comes down from the hills and swirls into the salt of the sea.

In the museum, they take good care of the drum. They smear it with oil and turn up the air-conditioning. The old people used to make a new drum when the old one fell apart. This drum is the last drum and must be kept away from the coast, away from the shacks of the old people, which do not have climate-control and adjustable lighting. Fair enough. The drum can stay where it is. The old people stay where they are.

Maika came that night, then went away again. She swept the men on the jetty into the sea, and then she gave them back again. That was Maika's will.

So much has happened since, but as to cause and effect, questions still hang in the air. Maika came back, and this time she stayed.

Maika returned and filled the whole bay. She settled, and as she came to rest, she threw fish high out of the sea and they rained down far inland. Maika lay down in this place, like a god, and look, you can see her eight arms, how they plug up the rivers that used to flow down to the sea. Shells lie where they fell, pushed into high mounds, heaped in waves on the former shore. The sea now pounds on reefs far, far away.

Maika settled and stayed. Where once the rocks were exposed at high tide, now Maika covers them with her white, translucent flesh. Her body stretches to the distant headland. The jetty stands, uprooted, across the giant's back.

Each day the flesh becomes firmer and darker, until you can walk across to the other side of the bay. The children bounce over, *boiing boiing boiing*, but the old people are more respectful and watch where they put their feet. Some places are slippery, where water still lies, and salt encrusts the high plateau.

Maika is changing from one state of being into another, from god to land. At night, she glows with phosphorescent light. If you climb the cliffs, you can see the new night-lights, stretching west far inland along ancient river beds, glowing east from here to the horizon.

Ant, spider, crab, and starfish find new habitats. The turtles that once swam to graze the sea grass meadows must give this place a miss, now that the sea meadows are history.

The jetty juts out over land. Its foundations are not firm.

Maika roamed the seas. She came to a place she liked and lay down and became land.

The old sea markers are gone, but that is the way of the sea. Once there were roads in the sea, and the old people slipped their canoes along tidal currents through mangrove flats.

The sky signs remain, but the sea signs are gone. Headlands become hills, beaches lie stranded far from the sea, swamps are born anew in the places where Maika stretched out her arms, as fresh water forces new paths.

The smell of the sea has left this place.

Soon the real estate fellas will come. Maika has changed from god to land and back to god again, in their way of looking at it, at their gods of what is bought and what is sold. What was once sea has become land, and public rights to the sea will not prevail. Their mob still owns this, from the ancient shore to the horizon. Land, sea, doesn't matter. Now they know it, the government mob and their lawyers. Now they come north with papers to be signed.

Sea rights become land rights, and land rights may be sold. See these papers, note their promise of great riches. Sign here, at this place.

The old people say they never learned the ways of signing papers. Sorry.

The matter of sovereignty will be solved. One day, a new city will be built.

They will drill canals through to the distant sea, and beside the canals the land will be carved into lots. Mansions will rise, each with its personal jetty, though the foundations will have to be drilled deep and piles pushed into the bedrock far beneath. New roads will lead to the city. Development will bring its own rewards.

Maika came, and stayed, but only for now. Her time here will pass, and one day she will arise and move on somewhere else. They will call it earthquake and tsunami. The mansions will crumble to dust and the canals yield up their niche inhabitants, the crocodiles and bull-nose sharks, to lie in the air, surprised, and for the moment lost for evolutionary inspiration.

Maika will rise and slide out of the bay, just as once she entered it. Her arms will curl in toward her belly, drawn from the buried beds of fossil rivers. Her eyes will open, and her gaze will be fixed on the ocean depths, where the fumaroles smoke and the hydrothermal trenches guard the magma sheath beneath.

One day, Maika will have had enough. She will call to the deep, to her mother, and her mother will call to her, "Come." What is sea will once more become land; what is land will become sea. Maika will say, our time has come, my mother, my sisters. The gods will walk over the waters, but where they make their home anew, they will choose to change it to suit themselves, and the oceans will rise, and rise, and the land will build up, but this time beneath the sea, and no one will own the sea, from here to the horizon. No one will own the land.

All will be sea, and the gods will, once more, come rightly into their own.

Books
by Rosaleen Love

If Atoms Could Talk, Greenhouse
  Press, Melbourne, 1987.

The Total Devotion Machine and Other Stories,
  The Women's Press, London, 1989.

Evolution Annie, The Women's
  Press, London, 1993.

*Reefscape. Reflections on the Great Barrier
  Reef*, Allen and Unwin, Sydney, 2000 and
  Joseph Henry Press, Washington DC, 2001.

"Ursula K. Le Guin and Therolinguistics"
Rosaleen Love's study of therolinguistics is an act of homage to...Ursula K. Le Guin's "The Author of the Acacia Seeds." ...Love borrows Le Guin's premise to create a worthy (and hilarious) companion piece, managing at the same time to critique the original story, the conventions of nature writing, and poststruturalist literary theory.
    —Brian Attebury, *Paradoxa*

"Once giants roamed the earth"
This story is informed with deep concern for the beauty of the earth and speaks urgently for respect and dignity. There is an air of menace and yet a pervasive hum of hope. The writing is firm, confident and compelling.
    —Carmel Bird

"The Total Devotion Machine"
Displaying a breathtaking ability for lateral thinking, Love takes many familiar science fiction themes...and twists them together with strands from the history of science and technology, classical and aboriginal mythology, power play and foibles from academe, and, most important, deep irony and flights of fantasy.
    —Peter Taylor, *Science, Technology and Human Values*

Evolution Annie
Imaginative, funny, spirited, subversive, many of these stories explore and play with gender and gender roles in one way or the other. The title story sets the stuff about Man the Hunter and the Ascent of Man and all that on its ear.
    —Ursala K. Le Guin

"The Raptures of the Deep"
... At once ominous and threatening...one the finest pieces of weird fiction ever written by an Australian, and shows Love's deep understanding of the geography of anxiety.
    —Jonathan Strahan, *Locus*

About the Author

Rosaleen Love is an Australian writer who enjoys playing with wild ideas from both science and feminism. She has a special love for the sea and its stories, and a soft spot for tales about impossibly large sea monsters with political ambitions.

A short story writer, she has published two collections with the Women's Press, UK: *The Total Devotion Machine* (1989) and *Evolution Annie* (1993). Her work has been included in mainstream as well as science fiction anthologies in Australia, Britain, and the USA, e.g., *Heroines, Millennium, The Art of the Story, Coast to Coast, The Women's Press Book of New Myth and Magic, Alien Shores, Metaworlds, She's Fantastical, Women of Wonder, Dreaming Down Under, Women of Other Worlds, Earth is but a Star, Year's Best Fantasy 2003,* and *The Elastic Book of Numbers.* She is also a science writer and writes on Australian science and society with a particular interest in coral reefs. Her non-fiction book *Reefscape,* a series of essays on the meaning of the Great Barrier Reef, was published in 2000 by Allen and Unwin, Sydney, and in 2001 by Joseph Henry Press, USA. She is never happier than when immersed in warm reef waters.

Once she was a university teacher, first in the history and philosophy of science, and later in creative writing, at Swinburne and Victoria Universities, Melbourne. Currently she is a research associate at Latrobe and Monash Universities, Melbourne. For a while, she was even in demand as a futurist, despite her own sense of helpless ignorance about the topic. Futurists, however, are wild people who like wild ideas, and for a while, she felt quite at home in their company.

Printed in Great Britain
by Amazon

42340408R00067